Y0-BBX-667

Praise for J. Boyer's previous collection
of short stories, *Desert Ice*

*"Exploring the nuances of family life, Boyer writes with
searing intelligence. His stories roar with emotional power,
but it's the quiet, probing intensity of characters trying to
locate their place in the world, trying to give voice to their
deepest fears and desires, trying to uncover as well as sus-
tain intimate bonds where Boyer proves himself to be the
master storyteller. DESERT ICE is a book of our time
— to be read and reread."*

Jewell Parker Rhodes, author of *Ninth Ward*, winner of the 2011 CORETTA SCOTT KING
BOOK AWARD.

*"The technical execution in these interrelated stories is mas-
terful and breathtaking. J. Boyer's look at love and marriage, at family, haunts beautifully throughout, and the
wisdom which courses through these pages enriches the soul.
These are stories for those who know: in the lives of others,
we see best and recognize, come to know, our own humanity. J. Boyer's treatment of humanity in DESERT ICE
is both sorrowful and magical. A work of grace."*

T.M. McNally, author of *The Goat Bridge*, finalist
for the PEN/FAULKNER AWARD.

*"DESERT ICE brings us fiction at the ever-moving edge of who we are today – as we work to invent care and to survive the perilous and deceptive adventures of love and – dare I say it – family. Sometimes we ice skate in the desert just full of hope as the past slides into the future. J. Boyer's stories ring with offhand wisdom and fresh drama – and a wondering and abundant affection."*

Ron Carlson, author of *The Signal*, Director, University of California/Irvine Creative Writing Program

*"J. Boyer's DESERT ICE is a sophisticated, urbane concatenation of fictional islands, delicately linked, from person to person, from childhood to senescence. Unfolding in Cape Cod, New York City and Arizona, these are stories of relationship, of parenthood and marriage, marriage a corrosive stability where the open-ended possibilities of youth are replaced by accumulated disappointments and deadening endurance, as well as by the bittersweet of repetition and the rare, resurgent surprise of love. DESERT ICE is an understated, irresistible call of wisdom — to celebrate in the midst of, and in spite of, difficult truths and to accept the ways in which human connection, sudden or sustained, can both enervate and renew our lives."*

Melissa Pritchard, author of *Late Bloomer* and *The Disappearing Ingenue*

# FLIGHT

A Short Story Collection

**J. Boyer**

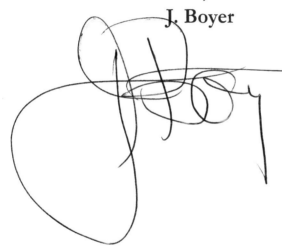

Fomite
Burlington, Vermont

Copyright © by J. Boyer

All rights reserved. No part of this book may be reproduced in any form or by any means without the prior written consent of the publisher, except in the case of brief quotations used in reviews and certain other noncommercial uses permitted by copyright law.

This is a work of fiction. Names, characters, places and incidents are either the product of the author's imagination or are used fictitiously. Any resemblance to actual persons, living or dead, events or locales is entirely coincidental.

ISBN-13: 978-0-9832063-7-8

Library of Congress Control Number: 2011943864

Fomite
58 Peru Street
Burlington, VT 05401
www.fomitepress.com

Cover: Sculpture by Peter Schumann, Bread & Puppet Museum, Glover, Vermont, Photograph by Donna Bister

FOR ELISSA,

MAY YOU CONTINUE

WRITING GOOD STORIES

FOREVER

Joy

February
2013

FOR SOPHIE AND ROANNE

## ACKNOWLEDGEMENTS

All but one of the twelve stories in this collection have been published earlier, "Wollicott's Traveling Rabbit's Foot Minstrels," which was originally conceived as a work for the stage and published as a full-length one act play in Canada by One Act Play Depot in 2002, then in this country went on to win the 2005 Theatre Publicus Award for Dramatic Literature. As for the rest, some have been published several times, some in America, some abroad, some both, and most in a slightly different form. "Flight" first appeared in *The Copperfield Review*, April, 2005; the first North American publication of "The Night Mechanic" was in *Ploughshares,* Volume 32, Number 4, Winter, 2006, but its initial publication was in Great Britain in *Anthology of 2004 Biscuit Prize Poetry and Fiction Winners* subsequent to being Finalist/With High Commendation for the 2004 Biscuit Prize For Fiction, and after its appearance in *Ploughshares* it was translated into Farsi by Asad Amraee and published as a chapbook, *Mekanik E Shabkar Asgeqameh I Dram Dar Dar Fasl E Kootach*, Eshigh Publications, Tehran, Iran, June, 2007; "Vivienne" first appeared in *Paradigm*, Issue 3, Summer, 2008, then was later collected in *Paradigm Volume II*, ed. Paul Fuhr, Columbus, Ohio: Rain Farm Press, 2009; "The Musical Afternoon Of An Odd November Day" in Great Britain in Edge Hill College's literary magazine *The Black Market Review*, Volume I, March, 2009; "The Fattest Woman On Earth's Near Death Experience..." was first published in *Midwest Literary Magazine*, February, 2011, then it was anthologized in *Winter Canons*, ed. Anthony Shields; "Love In The Time Of Paris Hilton" appeared in *audience*, Volume 4, Number 1, Summer, 2009; "29 Novembar Street" was published in *Just West Of Athens*, Winter/Spring, 2007; "The Year That It Rained" was published in Australia's *The Blue Crow*, Volume 2, October, 2010; "A Reversal Of His Fortunes" was first published in Turkey in the *Istanbul Literature Review*, Winter, 2006 and was later anthologized in *Pulp*, ed. Chris Gabrysch, Dallas: Twit Publishing, 2011; "The Secret

Lives Of London Detectives" was published in Algeria in *The Arabesques Review*, Volume 1, Number 2, March, 2006; "The Falconer" was first published in Great Britain's *Gulper Eel*, July, 2010, and was then anthologized in *The Seventh Deadly Sin*, ed. Christopher Jacobsmeyer, New York: Shade City Press, 2011. Many of these stories were drafted while the author was in Europe, all were drafted while the author was given time away from his teaching in the Creative Writing Program of Arizona State University, and virtually all were written while the author was living on financial grants. There were several granting agencies, but primary among them was the Virginia G. Piper Foundation. The author is very grateful for these initial publications, not to mention the financial support that made so much of their writing possible. He is indebted to each, and to all.

# CONTENTS

# PART ONE

# Flight

The walk she took up and down Bath's Kingsdown Hill was ever-so beautiful, which Rosalind found occasion to remark on several times, and the walking partner who had been arranged for Rosalind by her solicitor Mr. Dymer was very companionable in this regard, each time agreeing that it was certainly a lovely day, adding once a few remarks about a smarter resort up the coast he knew of, leaving her believing by the end of their outing that not only had it been a beautiful day and a beautiful walk but also an unexpectedly long one, as well as leaving her feeling at the moment that hers was a mind struggling against lost hopes and low spirits, like someone willing herself into a serious illness while everything about her person was well, as if she were hurrying herself to some tepid old-age actually, eager to reach the point when she could look back on this period as her *autumnal years*, to wit, a time of no particular pleasant — much less happy — event. Then all that would be left her to do before going to her grave was to accept the woman she'd become and no doubt been meant to be to begin with, a woman who having raised her family was now unequal to her husband and unwelcome to her children, *a woman alone*, to wit.

And as for Mr. Dymer, where was he as all of this was transpiring, and was he upset as well? He was. He certainly was indeed, for he'd been from governmental office to governmental office still wearing his moth-holed, blue Kent running shirt after going for his jog. He'd agreed to finalize her divorce papers just as she'd asked, but what he hadn't foreseen was that a clerk he was expecting to find at his desk was out sick for the week with croup and a headache. In the clerk's place was someone who didn't know heads or tails about the duties before her. A little whiff of a thing, she'd been trained at an estates agency and could distinguish between a sell and a let, no doubt, but could not distinguish at all between a High Bench stamp and anything else. She gave a very favorable account to this Dymer of a twin-gabled house in his neighborhood that was going for a song as she hunted through an octagonal box of stamps and sealing wax, complaining that her mother, a woman who was as amiable in public as she was disagreeable at home, had fitted her out as a child in thick grey flannels of that prickly material, which explained why she never wore flannel today, and why her mother and she had very little to say to one another, but she did not, in the end, find the seals or the stamp he required, and the solicitor left her company not one bit better off than when he'd begun. So there was Dymer, who thought he knew every civil servant in the resort town of Bath, Dymer who specialized in quickie divorces, some "quickie-er" than others apparently, feeling depressed and fidgety, thinking he'd have to come back late that afternoon when the little ninny was away for a tea, wondering what he'd say to Rosalind in the meantime, with no hint at all that his client could fly.

Raised near Stratford-On-Avon, midway as the crow wings between Warwick Castle and Shakespeare's home and birthplace, Rosalind had been fat and fair as an infant then become a thin and sickly child with wan cheeks and shrewd eyes and pale unblemished skin, the third child of five and the family's only daughter, a sensitive and clever girl who was amiable but quiet, gifted in the sciences, her parents suspected, but somehow unrealistic and therefore lacking what was needed to channel gifts into grades. She was only a passable student, and while unremarkable in any number of ways as well, she had discovered at the age of ten that she could hover several inches off the ground for moments at a time for no more trouble than closing her eyes and willing her arms into furious, breathtaking rhythms. This caused her to be removed from the earth, not far at first, of course, but later, with practice, allowed her to hover midair for moments at a time like a hummingbird might before a flower's full blossom. This, she did not disclose. A ten-year-old wants nothing more than to be like every other child her age, after all, for this is a time when other little girls named Thais or Andromeda demand of friends and family alike to be called Tiffany or Nancy Jo, and boys who can translate Homer with the skills of savants would much prefer dribbling a football, hence, she kept this to herself. No ten-year-old likes being a freak to their friends or a parlor trick to parents, particularly a British girl in a plaid school blazer with bands on her teeth and a brother who enlists in the Navy, and as the years went on, she found herself taking flight only when it was safest to do so, always when she was completely alone with no chance of detection, and generally when she felt quarrelsome to a great degree or thought there was nothing wrong with being unrealistic since her life seemed so hopeless and bleak, this often having to do boys unaware of her presence on earth with whom she had fallen in love, or, predictably enough, her own mother.

By twenty, she was earthbound, and married to a draftsman. A mother herself by twenty-two, twice again by the age of twenty-five. And by thirty, thirty-five, all thoughts of flight were forgotten, so overcome was she by children and husband both. When she met him sober and sensible, her husband became ambitious, optimistic and gregarious, rising in the architectural firm for which he worked, joining health clubs, entertaining, a man who spread his affections thin, as if their value increased for being so widely affordable, while her teenage daughters, as stubbornly themselves as silver-winged ponies, and at least as full of their own lives, were self-consumed and demanding, and with so many voices to be heard from, this became another silence in her own, as fully out of mind as to have never been thought to begin with.

Once the girls were married, her husband suffered headaches, backaches and spasms. From a stoic family, he suffered stoically and as a consequence seemed surprised to receive so much attention from his children each time he received it. She recalled how his suffering was so great toward the end of their marriage that he would have to go directly to bed, particularly after eating a hearty evening meal it had taken hours to prepare, announcing in an animated voice as he climbed the stairs that it had been the single best meal of his life, if he never ate again he'd still fared better than most, which, she should have seen, was simply to tell her he was lovelorn, a penitent. Or he might decide on a walk after dinner, so as not to be a bother to her, and sometimes, confiding he was fearful for his life itself, he'd feel compelled to return to his office to put the finishing touches on a blueprint, so that should he die in the night all could go ahead as planned without him. She could forgive him all that, she supposed, though she did wish the reason he'd withdrawn from her had been more than a simple affair, particularly one with his secretary. A middle-aged man with a wandering eye. His secretary? It seemed so uninspired, for the woman was half his age, a widow with children, who read him plays aloud in bed, romances chief among them, apparently believing while architecture was the agency of permanence it was fiction one looked to as the agency for change. Had Rosalind learned of this earlier, Rosalind would have met with the woman over lunch and explained to his secretary that not only could she have him if she was sure he was who she wanted, Rosalind would be only too happy to throw in their cottage, which, like him, was old and not in very good repair. Though the woman should then understand that she couldn't bring him back.

Rosalind boarded a bus, in any case. On impulse, she boarded a bus rather than return to her hotel room and ring up her solicitor and find herself divorced, particularly after such a long, long walk on such a beautiful day, and rode it past the Bath city limits to a spot from her honeymoon she meant to revisit, the Roman remains of a promontory, as well as one particular event she meant to revisit, then sat on a hill, spending the good part of an hour looking down on the resort town of Bath where people walked, incapable of getting things wrong, apparently, for life was always so easy.

Still wearing her wedding gown, she'd left him alone in their honeymoon suite, slipping away as he bathed himself for bed. Helping herself to a bike behind the hotel's dismal kitchen, she'd ridden in a panic here to this point, the highest she could reach without bursting a lung. What a sight she must have been in that gown! Where had she perched? Over there? What remained of the promontory was on the edge of things, and she moved her eyes to where a creek made a strange figure-eight of grey water and brown mud and slowed to a trickle as it curved through the silty brown then faded into the shadows that were thrown by the trees. The creek then ran south toward a ditch that was hidden by a canopy of overhanging branches that arched toward the sky from two banks, meeting in the middle as if reaching for the clouds. Never had a woman wanted wings so much as she had that night. Why had she not taken flight? For fear of the fall? The weight of the gown?

Later she walked the fields below. She combed them, thinking to herself that she could have survived a fall had it come, the fall was not nearly so dreadful as it had seemed in the dark. What was really dreadful, at the moment at least, was the rest of her life. A settlement, no matter how equitable, left a woman her age disadvantaged, as if it were a law of nature that women of sixty who were left on their own after years of married life must have a chromosomal propensity to live as modestly as possible. Then too there'd be her daughters. When they were young, she feared some horrific accident might befall her girls and she'd find herself surviving her children. What if she now survived their affection? Would she be expected to endure with a warm heart and a smiling face their concern for her welfare, her, a woman alone? Would she be required to make resolute statements about her health and well-being? Her diet? She could do without their quiet supervision, testing to see if her energies flagged. Would she find upon coming to their houses now that they'd invited an elderly man to be her dinner companion, or worse, when later he dodged a second invitation would there be affectionate jokes about her having broken the heart of her suitor, as if she wasn't their mother but instead a maiden aunt?

Climbing back to the top of the hill, flushed but by no means extended, thinking the world saw her now as the sort of woman for whom a companion is suggested when it comes to mind that she might take a walk to get her thoughts off her troubles, she made one last try at finding out what could possibly have possessed her to become enamored of her husband in the first place or to have lived her life as she had, the way a girl might have brought various rows of figures into random conjunctions as she learned to master a slide rule, without knowing a way to prove the solution without using the slide rule itself.

The bus ride back seemed twice as long as the bus ride going. Walking she thought might be preferable. In the work of a moment she lowered the thin upper section of the window letting in a quartering gale that caused a few of the passengers behind her in the rear to mutter to one another and buffet their hats with their hands. The air was cold against her cheeks. She reached into her bag for a scarf, which she tied beneath her chin. Feeling as if she had felt gravity's effects only too gravely, she felt as well a buzzing which ran along the skin of her forearm, then a sting. What stung, she supposed, was how her husband had broken the news, for he'd broken the news that he wanted a divorce by putting all the blame on himself, telling her now that their children were grown and with families of their own, he'd lost all interest in marriage, when, in fact, what he'd lost interest in was being married to *her*.

No, what had stung her was only a bee which had been sucked inside the bus when she'd opened the window. Husbands she thought were a bore, as was most of what was good for you, including fresh air and exercise.

The bus returned Rosalind to the area of her hotel and after that, and when it was quite dark, on her way to her quarters she passed a lounge near the gift shop where a little strain of music seemed to tremble like the flame of a candle and she recalled a long-forgotten tea she'd taken in that very room, or one very much like it, a honeymoon's bride. Sitting in shadowy solitude were several of her fellow hotel guests, only two of them at the same table, a pair of women in high spirits and very good color, an older woman and a girl who was saying "Is there nothing, aunt, I might do —" until her eyes met Rosalind's, at which time she looked at Rosalind stubbornly and refused to complete her thought. Rosalind took a table of her own. Her table was in the corner, as far away from the women engaged in their animated conversation as she could choose. She ordered an Amaretto but before it came changed her mind, asking for a double whisky instead. This was served to her by the bar man himself, put out apparently that he'd poured one drink and then been asked to pour another.

It was in this self-same room she took her breakfast in the morning. While buttering a piece of wafer-thin toast, she found herself being approached by a man. She thought she recognized him from the night before as a man who had begun to light a cigar and been told by the bar man, "None of that, sir, not in here. You'll have to take it outside, I'm afraid." He came toward her in degrees, then changed his mind, she could see, as if he had meant to meet one woman at her table and had found Rosalind there instead, then doubled back and in little more than a whisper said, "Rosie?"

She searched his face. "Do I know you?"

"Why, my God, it *is* you, Rosie. How long has it been?"

"Wally?"

"How good it is to see you after all these years. Do you mind if I sit down?"

"Of course not. Please do."

"Where was it Rosie, Ipswich or Dublin?"

"Brighton, I think."

"The Palladian porch. You're right."

"And there were glow worms that night."

"In the lane."

"Didn't you have a stammer?"

"With you I might have. No girl had ever scared me before. Are you still keen on gardening?"

"I haven't gardened for years. Forgotten I ever had, actually, until you just mentioned it."

They had met one summer when Rosalind was seventeen and Wally a year or two older, a point in their respective lives when nothing could have been more *dreadful* than a holiday with one's parents. So dreary are such times that a girl of seventeen is prone to falling in love with the first boy who asks her to dance, since so much of the work of a romance can be done in her head. In Wally's case, however, it was little short of chopping firewood. He'd been barely five feet tall and made up for this by the single most overwhelming ego of any boy his age. He'd looked down on her as if from on high, teasing her about her figure, dismissing what she had to say as if it were as light as air, criticizing her outfits as clothes for the needy. He was ferociously condescending at a time when she felt at once half-done and unsteady, remote when she was needy, ignored what she had to say as thin and impractical, and told her to behave like a grownup but affirmed that she had only once it was clear to them both she'd behaved like a child and given him his way. He was, in every form she could recall, insufferable. He was pig-headed, and self-concerned, and loud in ways which could drive one to distraction, incapable of delight for anything she had to say which he had not thought of first, and even if he had been rich and handsome — which, of course, he was neither — she could not see why any girl in her right mind would have given him so much as the simple time of day.

He was, in other words, the first boy she'd cared for. Ever.

"You can't remember the jetty."

"Of course I do. It was famous. You were short and wore bow ties and were generally impossible."

"I don't think that's so!"

"Being short, or impossible?"

"No, wearing bow ties. You, I recall, were thin as a pole."

"Yes. I was, you're right. But *you* were disagreeable. Well? Admit it."

Pity the poor woman who is never looked at the way Wally just looked at her. For every woman, at least once in her life, should feel so adored. "Ah, the same old Rosie," he said. "You don't know how many times I've thought of that summer."

"I've often wondered what became of you as well, Wally."

No, she did not re-marry. They spent a very pleasant morning instead in one another's company, and never saw one another again. For if a woman who divorces at sixty does not look forward to the autumn of her life, neither does she care for a second chance at spring. She's much too wise about the pass of the seasons.

After suffering a stroke the next year, Rosalind was sent by her daughters to Castringham Home, a misdirected attempt on the part of Prince Charles to preserve an ever-increasing population of pensioners, while also preserving Bath's architecture. Rosie was just such a pensioner.

And what became of Rosie, the heroine of our story? Some of the nurses say in the last months of her life she became slow of mind and fearful of anything feathered, while others say, quite to the opposite, actually, she went through long demented periods during which she tried to flap her arms and fly, twice jumping from an odd turret affair between the second and third stories of a freshly added annex. One goes so far as to report she succeeded, if only momentarily. It's still there, I believe, that turret. But none of the rest can be verified, and the majority opinion among those who remember her at all is that she enjoyed what is commonly known as a "western outlook," meaning, I suppose, a belief that the sun sets in the west when and how it chooses, and there's little to be done to effect either one, hence, one simply stands one's ground for as long as one can. She was then, by most common report, a modest, unassuming woman whose heart had never been broken, and whose death was of no particular consequence to anyone but those she left behind. Someone not given to flights of great fancy, certainly; I dare say, someone not given to any flights at all.

## The Night Mechanic:
## A Romance Novel in Ten Short Chapters

### Chapter One

One day — taken by the lilt of his wrists and the most beautiful hands she had ever seen on a man — she impetuously threw in her lot with a deaf and dumb mechanic who'd been deaf and dumb from birth. She fell in love as she was watching him sign, after meeting him in a garage one day, and after this they lived together in poverty in a succession of rented cottages in the small and still smaller villages of northwestern Scotland until finally they came to light near Northrup's Weir, only for her to discover in a state of generally failing health that her health wasn't failing at all, she was dying of one of those vague but specific diseases for which medicine knows no cure.

So there they were, our dying woman and her deaf and dumb mechanic, in a cottage near Northrup's Weir, and a pretty poor cottage at that.

### Chapter Two

There's never one unhappy person in a troubled relationship, always two, and never is this more the case than when one of the two is dying. She saw to that. She spent her days toward the end writing him sad little love notes and fashioning awful little dolls from bits of wool and twists of paper which she made him promise he would bury beside her. When he brought her a fork to eat with, she bent it: forks were for those with their health. It was almost as if she were angry that he might survive her, for she cast herself now in the role of someone trying to slip over the edge of a raft so as not to be a burden in a cold and choppy sea, which was to say that no matter how fast he rowed it could never be fast enough to save her, and Frank was meant to see this. Measuring out her dosages before leaving one night for work, he secreted the wish that she either recover miraculously before he returned or drown in her sea and be done with it.

## Chapter Three

There was no reason to suppose that he could help her save her life by embracing his own, yet he felt as if he might, and with a burst of energy he began this procedure as if it could all be done by the sweat of his brow. After scrubbing the cottage from top to bottom and replacing a broken drain spout, he gave it two coats of paint, and with that out of the way, he borrowed books from the library. He read a chapter a day for a week. He bought a new pair of trousers and drew up a list of a hundred-and-forty-seven things that might make him more appealing, some of them purely ridiculous, such as "MORE TALK" or "PUT A TWINKLE IN YOUR EYE." He tried to think of other things as well, but he was out of his depth, and when the rest of the month went by without a sign of her improving, he began to suspect that the efforts he was expending were of complete indifference anyway and he'd been foolishly wasting his time.

## Chapter Four

To conceal the taste of her fate, Frank, our mechanic, regularly served her tea in bed braced with teaspoons of whisky when he brought her her medicines, and showered them both with the odd little gifts of someone unfamiliar with how money can be spent, thinking, So much for economy, using the last of what they'd thought of as their savings on matching little things like silver-plated pencils and fur-collared coats.

Her sickness had spread through their rooms, edging him out, as a sickness sometimes does when there's no real hope for recovery, and now it was only before their listless kitchen heater that he felt fully in possession of himself or anything else, and the greying sky outside did nothing to increase his cheerfulness one morning when she called for a pot of tea. He offered biscuits as well, for her strength. He counted out two out of habit, though there was money for more. Putting the kettle on to boil, he took a glass from the cabinet, poured himself – measured himself, more properly – a full three inches of whisky, drank it straight down, then drank from the bottle itself, burning his gums and his tongue. That they'd lived hand to mouth for so long when there was money available began to seem like something she'd done to betray him, rather than a fate they had suffered in common.

She refused the biscuits he served on a tray. Too delicate now for cake, she asked him to boil her an egg instead. It took forever to fix it. He pointed toward the book she'd been reading, meaning, Is it a love story? "It might be," she answered, "if someone would die." Later, holding her hand in both of his own, he explained the delay.

## Chapter Five

The garage where he worked had the flyblown air of a business that is going down and Cal, its owner, who liked to date the milestones of his life by the few times he'd shown a profit, "Let me see now, I've had two operations and three kids since that year we were flush with cash," was always going on about having to fold his tent and move on if things didn't pick up very soon, but there was no more chance of that than of Cal sprouting wings. He'd been saying he was going broke for more than thirty years. To make ends meet, Cal kept the garage open round the clock working sixteen hours out of twenty-four, seven days a week. The less money the Scottish have the less inclined they are to set a table and spend it on food, so his wife, a sharp featured woman with frail bluish teeth, brought him his meals there, generally white bread and margarine, stewed beef, sugared tea and potatoes, whether this was breakfast, lunch, or dinner, so, reasonably enough, there was generally a whiff of meat fat in the office, rather than of rubber, petrol, and lubricants. It never quite smelled right to Frank, a mechanic. There shouldn't be air you could taste. You walk into a garage and garage smells should hit you in the face with a smack. It never quite felt right either. Working for Cal hadn't felt right since the day he went to a box of second hand distributors and found instead of distributors a pudding basin, three unopened bottles of Worcester Sauce, and two dirty cups. Nevertheless, the garage was as near as Frank had to a lifeline at the moment, helping to keep him afloat.

## Chapter Six

Fridays were slow as a rule. Cal was generally out of

tobacco toward the end of each week, but lit or not, Frank expected each Friday to get to the door and find on the other side the sunken cheeks of Cal's childish face as Cal drew on one or another of his ragged briar pipes, turning the pages of his racing final as if paring the skin from a yellowish large potato. The only thing out of the ordinary was that as Frank arrived for work that Friday evening, one of the locals was unfurling an air hose after fixing a flat on his bicycle using a puncture repair kit. Frank waved as he opened the door. "Quite all right, thanks," answered the cyclist. "Take care with your fine coat there. Don't want it getting greasy. Dismal night to be on your bike." Frank's coat felt warmer for being called fine. The cyclist with grizzled hair and a clipped mustache had been a lower-grade civil official who had recently come down in the world and moved to Northrup's Weir where he'd opened a business. Frank didn't know his first name. Jencks was his last. He had something to do with insurance. Normally he would have ignored the man and he was glad that he didn't, since his coat felt better for being called fine.

Frank's first chore of the shift was to empty a trash barrel. Work orders were listed in the sequence they'd arrived in multi-colored chalks on a green slate board with a corrugated gutter. The air inside the shop was chalky. Almost like snow, the chalk in the air was firm and powdery and it covered the hard wooden chair. He put on fingerless gloves. A thin curtain of pipe smoke dulled the glass of the window that faced out toward the pump.

About work, Frank was preciously aware of something the rest of us take for granted, namely, that there's a point at which the work momentarily vanishes, you're completely at one with yourself, and there seems to be no possibility at all for error, so he looked forward to tinkering with the cars he'd find in need of his service that evening. He found the same kind of selfless precision in working with his hands that others might find in working with lace.

The first of the work orders was for a Jeep Wagoneer that was out in a bay with a lift. Someone had put so much sawdust in the transmission to keep it running that its transmission fluid was clogged with fruity-smelling solids. The bay was locked. He opened it with a key.

The Wagoneer was an ancient Hydra-Matic that had been designed as though it would never need repair, not even minor standard maintenance, for everything was difficult to reach or took seven steps to do. The transmission didn't even have a drain plug. To change the transmission fluid and filter he would have to loosen the pan and allow the fluid to spill out over the top of the transmission pan, which meant the fluid spilt over everything.

The transmission pan was held in place by two attaching screws at each corner. The first thing Frank had to do was to put a drain pan down on the ground under the corner he started with. He loosened the two attaching screws, a little bit for this one, then a little bit for the next. What he was trying to do was to loosen all the screws of the transmission pan so that the fluid would drain from the corner where the drain pan was waiting to catch it. When most of the fluid was drained in this way, he had to push up on the transmission pan with one hand, take out all the screws with the other, then lower the transmission pan with both hands, slide out from beneath the chassis, and dump what was left of the fluid that had settled near the bottom before he could clean and dry it.

He was cleaning the pan standing over a drain with a long red tube of India rubber in one hand and the pan in other when the car's owners arrived, tourists on holiday, Frank assumed. The man said to the girl, "Why won't you use a proper car instead of this junker, Nora?"

Dyed a bright polymer green, the girl's hair was buzz cut into a rectangle half an inch high and she brushed it with her fingers as she spoke, as if brushing this away. "Do you know what I make, working in a scent shop?"

## Chapter Seven

That was the night it happened. A Friday. Returning from work, he found her dead in their cottage. She had died that night in her sleep, not the girl who had looked to Frank as if she'd strayed from the mother ship, but the woman who Frank had once loved. Our mechanic beat himself about the head and shoulders — figuratively speaking — for the better part of that morning for having gone off to work and left her to die by herself in the middle of nowhere. Deciding shortly after the lunch hour that it was time to say goodbye, he stood on the threshold of the room where she lay. He pushed open the door. Entering the room, he realized the coverlet on his side of the bed was neatly turned back at an angle as if he'd been expected to spend the night there. The thought gave him goose-flesh. Seeing her lying there dead, he felt the same way he'd felt once as a child when he'd seen a naked man on a snowy cold day: it had made Frank glad for his clothes. He closed their bedroom door behind him. He shut it tight. No one was there to tell Frank that he couldn't go into the room again, of course, yet he had the feeling it would be wrong to do so. With his back to the door, he wanted so badly to scream at the unfairness of it all, and his limbs were suddenly leaden at the thought that he couldn't. To keep feeling in his toes as he stood there, he developed an exercise on the spot whereby he lifted his heels from the ground so that he was supported by the balls of his feet. Later he notified the authorities to come for her body.

## Chapter Eight

Grief's a mysterious agent. We find nothing so surprising as the ease with which death can rob of us of those we've loved, no thought more absurd upon losing someone we've loved than the thought that we'll never see them again, and for Frank she was even more real in death than she had been while she was dying. Once her body had been removed, death, her death at least, took on tangible dimensions, height, weight, mass, physical characteristics, where once it had stood just beyond the scope of any lantern they'd shone upon it, and he treated it as such for the rest of the afternoon. As if she were just away on a trip, her death became her absence. Frank arrived for work that night just as the sun was setting and his employer was hopping up and down in agony after walloping himself on the forefinger with an oily ball peen hammer. Frank was soon left alone. After slipping on a pair of overalls hanging behind the door, he emptied the trash, then spent the shift without so much as the hint of a customer.

Cal had sawed off the arms of the chair in the belief that arms made a chair more comfortable. A man might not leave a comfortable chair. Arms or no, Frank stayed in that chair all night, leaving it once to put out the trash and a second time at dawn to use the Men's. Taking the key ring from the wall, he went around to the side of the building at the end of his shift, where he washed his face with a fist of paper towels. To make sure no one slipped the key in their pocket and drove off by mistake, Cal had put a counterweight from a pair of Calvinist velveteen curtains on a huge metal ring. He would have done this for the Ladies as well, but women, reasoned Cal, wore dresses and skirts not trousers and coats. Men were the ones with real pockets.

## Chapter Nine

Cal came to relieve him at the usual time. "So?" asked Cal. Opening the cash drawer, he continued, "Nothing new? Things were more or less like always, then? You didn't burn down the place. It's still here. Poor comfort."

Shortly thereafter, brushing aside the wing of a crawling insect, Cal took a clipboard of parts orders from beneath a pipe rack that held three of his favorite sandblasted briars and inked in the blocks near the bottom. Frank watched as he did this. Cal had to labor to get the forms right. Like all artisans with permanently dirty hands, Cal had a peculiarly delicate manner of handling things, particularly all things confusing, as if he feared he might break them, the way a small-boned woman might handle a bird or a starving man might pick up a crumb, and, as consequence he had to labor over this more than most of us might. When a car pulled up at the pump, he said to Frank, "Her. It's her again. The pump, Frank. If it's not too much trouble."

The driver was giddy. She'd been drinking. Wondering to himself if the woman would make it home alive in the condition she was in, wondering if he would find her on his way home in a ditch, her windscreen a cobweb of shattered glass, and her son's eyes as lifeless in death as a pair of children's marbles, Frank filled the tank of her foreign sedan while the woman went inside to place a call to her girlfriend. Frank next did her windscreen, staring into the face of a sleeping child, her son. He tried to see the woman through the smoke-smeared glass of the garage itself. She was standing by the phone. The boy was waking up.

## Chapter Ten

While Frank made change in the office, she took the giant ring of keys that hung from the wall, then beat it like a tambourine, shouting, "Ole!" as she twirled.

Cal said, "None of that. Not in here."

Frank held out his hand, demanding the key ring.

"My but this thing is heavy, why's it so heavy, Frank?" she said as she returned it. "Are you cryin'? Why's the bloody fool carrying on so, Cal?"

Frank pointed toward her car.

"Darn! Look at that. Just let me get my hands on him, would you!," she answered, while outside, front and back, the windows of the Cadillac shot up and down in a strange bad-tempered dance.

## Vivienne

Tom fetched their drinks from the bar while Vivienne claimed their table, a pair of G and Ts, his choice clearly not hers, spending longer than was called for, she thought, with a pair of sloe-eyed barmaids, sisters, Viv supposed, one who seemed to be under the influence of a great narcotic and the other, judging from the vacancy in her eyes, steadfastly determined to avoid any serious thought, in need of a guardian, no doubt, not that Tom noticed, for she was wearing a low slung peasant blouse and clearly her vacant gaze was of more concern from Viv's vantage than it could possibly be from his.

"Is this where you come normally?" asked Tom.

"It's just in the neighborhood where I come to see the milliner. Well, yes, sometimes, sometimes I suppose I do, yes."

"Ah."

"Just *Ah*? Well? What do you think?"

"So you didn't just wander in here and make a scene the other day — I must say it has its allure."

"From how you were peering down that girl's blouse, I'd say it has more than one."

"Thank God at least it's not crowded. Cheers."

"To actually having an income. Do you mind if I take off my shoes, Tom? My feet, I swear, are killing me."

"Tell me how you found this fabulous den of iniquity, Viv. Then we can go on to the part where they called the authorities."

"What?"

"The Cox and Comb here."

"Blind luck. It found me, actually. I was looking through — Tom, are you listening?"

Tom's attention had fled. His cheeks looked suddenly sunken, his flesh pale, his eyes, like two dark orbs looking away from the door. She followed his eyes with her own. "Oh God," said Tom. "Don't turn. Pretend you don't see him. There's Pound. And Joyce both."

Viv noticed at the door an atrabilious looking man who having had too much to drink had acquired the judicious walk of someone whose legs are soon to turn to cork-screws. She said, "Isn't that —"

"Old Forster as well. Oh God, Viv, I told you not to look. Now they'll join us for sure. Dear Lord, take me now, Pound's come with friends. And some of them were at the Savoy this evening. That awful to-do for Forster, to which neither of us were invited."

"To which I was not invited you mean. Would you prefer I just slipped away?"

"It's too late, Viv. They see us. Just wave."

"What are we going to do now?"

"What can we do!"

Tom impressed everyone he met with his varied ambitions, his boundless energy, his mischievous Anglophile charm; yet Viv knew he spent much of his emotional life along the shoals of depression and dissatisfaction, for he showed a side of himself to Viv he kept carefully concealed from anyone else. A coldness. A kind of polar winter. He had no close friends, and while he liked to claim he could charm a tea kettle into dancing a jig, and for that matter probably could, Viv thought, Tom had charm instead of warmth, had none of Viv's sun about him, nothing warm, not even his smile. Like so many others who learn early in their lives that they are good at all they care to try, he secreted the belief there was really nothing worth being good at, and while this could manifest itself as dry wit or even ironic detachment, depending upon the situation it could also come across as being peevish and superior, even contemptuous, as if Tom felt wholly justified in shutting off his charm at a moment's notice and becoming remote from others and disdainful of the world.

At least there'd be Pound, she thought, Pound who had brought them together. She'd known Pound forever, it seemed. She would sit, much as she was sitting here in the Cox and Comb, listening to Ezra Pound go on about America as if he were an emissary from a grand and distant continent, a potentate from an exotic emirate, pleased by how lucid Pound was and open in his judgments to anything she proposed, thinking he was the one male creature she'd ever met who saw her in the same light in which she secretly saw herself, as a truly — if indefinitely — special being, possessed of an idiosyncratic beauty, charming, of course, very charming, with a keen, even fierce wit and unspoken power to fascinate, an estimation of Pound's all the more convincing for how long and how lightly he'd worn his good opinion of her — and then again, to her eye at least, how visibly.

Such was the pattern this evening in the Cox and Comb.

It began with Pound speaking about the Savoy as the first round of drinks was served by the barmaid, then saying how Tom and Viv had been missed, but Viv most of all, going on to say that Viv's capacity for charming a room full of strangers was as natural as it was rare, then continued in this vein until his voice dissolved into the sound of pub crawl laughter and music from the street. Tom was saying at the moment that the world is divided into only two classes that make any real difference, the good and the bad, and while he supposed Viv, as a woman, could not help but desire to be one of the former, for himself he preferred the alternative, since good people were inevitably afraid of bad ones while the reverse was almost never true, a situation leaving the bad among us with a distinctly upper hand, he thought.

Viv protested, "That's not what I meant, and you know it, Tom."

"Well that's certainly what it sounded like to me."

"Do you listen to anything I say, anything at all? Is there anything else I've done wrong?"

"Yes. Now that you bring it up. Your view of the world."

"My view of the world, is that all."

"Yes, Vivienne. Your view of the world."

To hear Tom tell it, she had opinions about nearly everything, some of them to be greatly improved had she by accident been given a brain, and, in any case, most of them what he called "fashionably out of step," for instance explaining away Lady Ottoline Morrell as being misunderstood by the public, when it was clear to anyone with even the hint of a pulse that the woman was pigeon-toed, ugly, and fat.

So clearly excluded was she now that Viv turned to

Tom's friend Pound and said, "Well? Save me."

They struck up a flirty conversation, as they were wont to do, with Viv hoping Pound might take up her part straightaway, which he did, calling to Tom at the other end of the table, first saying to Tom that he hadn't noticed Lady Ottoline Morrell being pigeon-toed but had thought to himself as Tom was making his case that were he Tom he would never be seen in public with someone as attractive as Vivienne, since considered in tandem they were very much like a flower pulled up with a handful of weeds, leaving it to Tom's imagination whether or not Tom was the flower, and adding that while a flower might be its own excuse for being, weeds were generally snatched from the earth by their roots and then chucked in a bin with the detritus and slops — or hadn't Tom noticed? To which others joined in like a chorus:

"Now there's a calling for you, Eliot: compost. If banking doesn't work out, you'll have an alternative."

"Yes, I can imagine Tom as compost."

"We all can."

"I must say he has the gifts for it."

To Tom's right sat E.M. Forster, a rumpled looking man in a worn tuxedo, who had he been a book might have surely been a dog-eared book, she was certain, and Mr. Dog-Ear leaned across to her to say, "Is he always this rude, Vivienne?"

"No. Tom's changed."

"Really?" said Tom. "I'd love to know how."

"Should I tell him?" Viv asked.

"Please do."

Before she could, someone said, "He used to be a ski

instructor."

Another added, "At San Moritz."

Then another: "A ski instructor named Ingrid."

"By God that's right, I'd forgotten."

"Don't you remember?"

Vivienne finally got a word in, saying, "I liked him better as Ingrid, actually."

"We all did."

"Right."

"Well."

"At least Ingrid knew her place."

Vivienne leaned into Pound and asked confidentially, "Who are these terrible people?"

"My supporters."

"Your what?"

"My supporters."

"Of which there seem to be plenty. All very male, and all of them drunk. Your supporters indeed, you sound like a politician."

Pound explained that he was taking Tom's poem "The Waste Land" from one publisher's office to the next and so strange was it all that he'd had to enlist the support of just about every literary luminary who still owed him a favor. He said to ensure the largest turnout possible he bribed anyone in Tom's favor with a pint of whisky to get them to write on the manuscript's behalf, and bribed anyone against Tom with a quart of the same, this in the hope it might make them too drunk to raise their voice or bother with pen and paper. That's how he got his own poems published, he said.

"Does it really work?"

"Every time."

"Are you that afraid you'll never publish again?"

"Just the opposite, confidentially. I'm scared silly I'll publish and be exposed as a fraud."

"You're not really lobbying publishers on Tom's behalf, are you?"

"I'm afraid so. It's like loading the gun with which he'll be shot. I suppose you think I'm foolish."

"I'm foolish as well. It's fine. Thanks for being a good sport about Tom's little scribblings. I'm not sure what we'd do without Tom to remind us of how unhappy we should be with the state of the world, or how foolish we must be to marry. Wives, Pound, there's the problem, they're distant and cold. And in my case, unstable."

"Thanks for the warning."

"You're very welcome."

"Tom just craves the limelight. He has a nose for it, actually. Look at him down there, holding court."

"You mean Tom's a social climber?" Viv asked.

Forster overheard this as he was returning from the loo and said in passing that Tom was thought by their friends to be the worst sort of social climber actually, which, in the circles in which they ran, was to say the most *obvious*, not the most avaricious or venal, since both avarice and venality were understood to be strengths of character by the true literati, though it seemed perfectly clear this was only the opinion of those who had met Tom in passing alone. In any case, it was perfectly absurd since social climbers were — by definition — eager for the good opinion of their social betters, always aping the ways and manners of those they admired, ever-eager to be acknowledged and noticed, while anyone with whom Tom was truly intimate recognized Tom was much too self-involved and too acutely self-absorbed to be aware of anyone but Tom himself, let alone concerned with their opinions or their place in the world.

"You sound stung from your tone. It's not that he's leaving you high and dry is it, and you'll have to replace him with another acolyte?"

"No, this I'm afraid is personal."

"Oh that sounds worse yet. He hasn't broken your heart, has he?"

"Broken my *what?*"

"I'll teach him a lesson, if he has. He's very attractive. Nothing to be ashamed of. Just because one has sex with men doesn't make them queer does it."

Pound said, "Really? It doesn't? Thank God. That's such a relief."

"It'll give us something in common. I've had sex with men more times than I can count. Does that make me a lesbian?"

"You're quite the flirt, Viv," said Joyce, taking a chair from another table and pulling it close to hers.

"Oh, I'm much worse than that. It's well-documented. I am positively mad and a consistent disruption to Tom and his art."

"Yes?"

"I make his life a perfect hell. Isn't that clear from what you've seen this evening?"

"Actually I thought you were flirting with me."

"Only because I was. I'm not wasting my time with you am I, you don't like boys?"

"*Moi?*"

"Toi."

"I can be easily won, if you're interested."

"I find I do best with the Irish when they share my liberal views. Yours aren't particularly liberal, I suppose."

"Not particularly."

Viv said, "No, I thought not."

"Your Tom's the worst sort of prig, you know that, don't you, Viv?"

"What?"

"Tom of course," said Joyce. "He's a prig. The worst sort, I was saying. Look at him now, laughing and joking. He's always laughing at something, or someone, your husband; it's no wonder, he's an American, loves re-inventing himself. The minute he has to face himself in a mirror, he wants to be someone else, and virtually anyone else will do. That's why he can't hold a job. The sad thing is he's completely conventional, the most ordinary person I've ever met, and he hasn't a clue at all that he is."

Vivienne cut Joyce off, saying they must be speaking of two different Toms, thinking to herself that for whatever reason Mr. Joyce here genuinely disliked her husband, and the truth was that Tom thought ill of him as well. She could not help but think that whatever had transpired to make them get under one another's skin this way spoke directly to her interests. Certainly it was helping to make Joyce attractive to her. Maybe dangerously so, for she went on to say that Tom was the least conventional person she'd ever met, but in a tone meant to let Joyce know that she was egging him on, for she could feel Tom's eyes upon them, glaring at them from the table's other end.

"What are you two whispering about?" called Tom.

"You're not seducing my wife, are you?"

"To the contrary," said Viv, "I'm seducing him." She took from her purse a pen and piece of paper. "See, I'm writing out my address and my phone number. I've been trying to get him to flee you literary cretins and come back to our place, but he's damnably resistant."

She slipped the paper before Joyce.

"What does it really say?" asked Tom.

Pound snatched the paper away, stood, and read it aloud: TO THE BEARER OF THIS NOTE. I WILL SLEEP WITH YOU ON THE PROVISION THAT YOU HELP MY HUSBAND PUBLISH HIS POEM THE WASTE LAND, SO AT LAST HE CAN BE DONE WITH THIS AND GET BACK TO HIS BANKING.

To the delight of them all, he made a show of slipping the paper straight to his pocket.

"Is that what it really says?" asked Tom.

"You're a cynic, Eliot," said Pound.

"If you ask me, you're the cynic at the table," said Tom. "You have to pretend life is elliptical in order to endure it, and if that's not cynical then I don't know what is."

"I'm not too cynical to let you buy the next round, Eliot."

"Nor I," said someone else.

"Here, here," said Dog-Ear.

"A toast to cheap happiness," said Viv.

"Made all the happier at *Tom's* expense," Pound added.

"Oh ye of simple faith," said Tom. "You see, Viv, you see what I've been talking about? They're sordid little creatures, the lot of them. And this, I'm afraid, is but the tip of the iceberg. Here, see if you can get that little whiff of a barmaid to come in our direction."

Leaving Tom and the others to their own, Viv returned to their flat, opened her closet, and took from a shelf a package of delicate votive candles she'd purchased along with espadrilles and chocolates in a market in Nice. She slipped out of her evening clothes and tried on several things hurriedly before deciding on what she should wear, then remade the bed from this morning. She would have done still more by way of preparation but there was a knock at the door, which caught her up short. She caught a glimpse of herself in the mirror, tried something with her hair and brought her face to her own reflection to inspect something about her mouth.

As she set the candles around her bedroom and lit them one at a time, she thought of the slip of paper on which she'd written where they lived in case drink had gotten the better of its bearer, who she knew would be Tom, since Tom was inevitably the last to turn his back on an evening but the first to be drowned by his cup.

There was a second knock, and she said she was coming. Then added, "Thank God you found your way. I felt like I was scribbling. And in the dark, no less. It's a wonder you could read it."

She took a deep breath before she opened the door, and when she finally did, she said, "Tom."

"Can I come in, Vivienne?"

"What are you doing here? Why aren't you still with your friends?"

Tom waited to see if she meant to block his way. When she stepped aside, he went directly to the bedroom. Discovering the candles, he said, "Expecting someone, Viv?"

"That's none of your business, Tom. You're drunk."

"I'm many things. Embarrassed. Betrayed. Humiliated."

Tom held out the slip of paper on which she had written their address. When she reached for it, he jerked it away. She reached a second time. Again, he put it out of her reach. "Give me that," she said.

He held it high over his head, as if he expected her to jump for it.

"You're pathetic. It's late, Tom. We'll talk about this tomorrow."

"Tell me, Viv. Was it fun? Did you enjoy it?"

"Did I enjoy *what?*"

"You know very well."

"What I do is none of your business."

"I hope you enjoyed it, I really do." He took her arm in his hand.

"That's my arm, Tom."

"So it is."

"Are you giving it back? May I have it?"

"Well? I'm waiting for an answer."

"If you're finished with it, I'd like it back. If it's not too much trouble."

Tom still had hold of Viv's arm, his grip growing tighter. Viv did her best to wrest it away. Tom grabbed her with his other hand to hold her still. She did her best to resist this as well, kicking at him and squirming, even trying once to bite him, until Tom let go entirely.

"You fight like a girl," said Viv.

"So do you."

"Look at these marks. Are you happy now?"

"Do we have anything to drink, Viv?"

"Damn you," she said. "That hurt. It still hurts."

"I don't care if it does."

Through the open door walked Pound.

"Well who do we have here?" said Tom. "The man of the hour."

"Are you all right, Viv?" asked Pound. "Your husband made the most goddam stinking scene once you left. I assumed he'd find his way home here, sooner or later."

Tom made a pitiable effort at sounding sober, and civil. Which in Tom's case generally meant *British*. He said, "You're not welcome here, Pound. It's best that you go."

Pound ignored this. "Let me see your arm, Viv. Why are you rubbing it?"

Tom tried to block Pound as he stepped forward, and the two men tussled for a minute. Pound got the better of it. He put Tom in a chair and told him to stay there. Tom said drunkenly, "Did you just put your hands on me? I'll kick your arse good, that's what I'll do. I demand that you leave. Immediately."

"Not until I'm certain she's safe. Let's see that arm, Vivienne."

"It was nothing," answered Viv.

Tom charged Pound from behind, leaping upon his back. Vivienne did her best to pry him free, saying, "You're only making this worse, can't you see?"

"Get off me, you fool, you're choking me," said Pound.

"You're both being perfectly ridiculous," said Viv.

Tom made a stupid cowboy noise, as if riding a bucking bronco. Then dismounted on his own and straightened his clothes. "All right, we're calm now. Order's restored. All's well with the world."

Pound said, "Sit down, Tom. Sit down and shut up.

There. There in that chair."

Tom missed the chair and collapsed. Pound knelt over him, and once he was sure Tom was fine, he asked Viv to help get Tom to the couch.

"Is he unconscious?" asked Viv.

Pound replied, "Nothing so dramatic. He just can't hold his liquor. He's done for the night. Here. Let's take off his shoes."

Viv removed one, while Pound removed the other. "Can I get you something?" she asked.

"No, it's late, I've got to be going."

Viv leaned her back against the door as she was showing him out. She took Pound's face in her hands and kissed him, sweetly at first, then deeply. She said that was his reward for standing watch over Tom.

Pound shook his head and began to laugh. "What do you hate most, Viv? That he has such talent? Or that he hasn't enough to do this without you? He wouldn't write if it weren't for you, you know, he'd be perfectly content as a banker. Is that why you keep things in constant turmoil?"

"Why, what do you mean?"

"*Why, what do you mean?*" said Pound, batting his eyes. Laughing darkly to himself as he descended the stairs, he called, "You're not crazy at all, are you, Viv. No, you're worse. You're awful, you're shameless. I've never seen anyone so ambitious. Jesus Christ, what a pair!"

# The Musical Afternoon of an Odd November Day

## BELGRADE, 1991

Crossing the bridge was madness. Still in uniform, a beetle-browed man, a frantic civil servant of some kind, shinnied up one of the bridge's suspension cables, then hand over hand he made his way forward above the crowd by negotiating the supports that held in place a huge sign commemorating the bridge's dedication. The sign, reading *BRIDGE OF BROTHERHOOD AND UNITY,* had never been meant to hold a man's weight, and it bent outward and away from the bridge, so that the man found himself dangling above the Sava River. He looked down at the water with surprise, as if he were thinking, Where did that come from, a river? Here? Why would there be a river *here?*

Menninger looked down at the water as well. The waters of the Sava were normally flowing. Today, they were inexplicably calm.

Albert Menninger looked up at the dangling man, then down to the water, as if all time had been stopped to the second, as if time itself had somehow been suspended. To Menninger, the water appeared lucid, frugal, calmly waiting for the body of a man it expected to drown. When he looked into the dangling man's face for one final glimpse, the man's eyes seemed confused. His feet flailed, as if solid footing on land were only inches away, then his fingers slipped and he plunged into the Sava. Then everything rushed forward at a lunatic, impossible pace.

Flight, smoke, flame, shot — you couldn't see where you were going — they ran together, they made no sense. Abandoned lorries and cars had been swallowed up by masses of people who were fleeing in panic from the troops and Milosevic's tanks. Unable to pull forward, the lucky drivers had gotten out from behind their steering wheels and joined the crowds on foot, forsaking their cars as they fled for the lives. From behind the wheel of hers, a woman trying to open the door said, "Get moving now! You don't understand who I am. Move along, God Damn You!" She seemed to be holding up a form of identification, a badge of some kind. There were places on the bridge where the crowd was surely a hundred men wide, shoulder to shoulder in either direction. Government police, soldiers of all ranks, some of them deserting perhaps.

In Student City, several hundred students had tried unsuccessfully to block the path of the incoming troops by commandeering buses, trucks, then mounting other forms of barricades. After several days of stand off, tanks were sent in to put an end to things. What had begun as an act of political courage for Menninger and his friends had touched off a firestorm. Now sirens wailed throughout the city. Every few minutes scattered explosions could be heard. Before getting to the bridge on the other side of the Sava, Menninger had faced advancing lines of government soldiers firing hundreds of rounds into cornered crowds of fleeing civilians. Now he faced a horse.

People tried to give the frightened animal a wide berth when it reared, but there was nowhere they could go. It came down directly on top of them, throwing its rider clear. Further along, Menninger came face to face with a heavyset man wearing only a short-sleeved T-shirt and American army fatigue pants. Menninger was still wearing his lab coat and the man asked, "Are you a doctor?" Menninger answered, "The University of Belgrade. I'm studying medicine." As he tried to squeeze past, the man grabbed Menninger by the shoulder and said, "You know, I have nothing against the SPO *or* the students. Actually, I rather like them, they make reliable part-time employees. Here, let me do you a favor." He pulled up his T-shirt and exposed his huge belly. Apparently he wanted Menninger to see his tattoo. The tattoo was of a naked woman reclining on her back. Her feet were flat, her knees were spread. The tattoo artist had aligned the ridiculous image so that the fat man's hairy naval became her genitalia. The fat man threw back his head and roared with laughter, wiggling her labia from side to side. Menninger did the best he could to get past.

He didn't succeed until he was pushed forward from behind. He almost fell and Menniger turned to see who he had to thank for this. A maid from the Hotel Voltaire had put on a full-dress military tunic, a formal uniform belonging to one of the guests, and now her chest was festooned with tiny medals. Beside her was the man who pushed him, a bearded man who had stolen a cheap print of the Mona Lisa from the lobby of the same establishment. He had cut out the face. In its place was his own, and he was balancing the painting's ornate gilt frame with one end in either hand. He spoke to Menninger as if he were proffering the young man the wisdom of the ages. "Go on," he said. "Get going.

This is just a drop in the ocean."

"Where did you come from?" asked Menninger.

"The Hotel Voltaire, where do you think?"

"Why somewhere so ritzy?"

"I just returned from the language school in Berlin," he answered in Yugoslavian. Then, in German, he continued his thought: *"Ich wusste noch nicht, dass die Stadt ein Schlachtfeld geworden war,"* I did not know that the town had become the battlefield.

Menninger asked, "Do you think we'll ever get across? I have to get across the bridge to Nyskli Hill. It's very important. The Erdoly-Palais?"

Perhaps the man trying to disguise himself as the Mona Lisa was only at this instant getting a good look at Menninger, for he answered, "Forget everything I just let slip. Strictly confidential. Just between the two of us. All we have is one another. Got it?"

At the edge of the bridge, the fleeing crowd spilled out onto the streets of the city, streaming past an elderly woman with badly dyed hair. She looked to be in shock. She held up a power plug attached to a length of electrical cord, as if a toaster might have been wrenched from her hands only moments before. There was something darkly, ludicrously festive in the air. There were occasional cheers, some singing. People who had struggled for their lives to get across the bridge now hugged one another. Menninger hadn't the time. He hurried up a side street then crossed over to a more heavily traveled boulevard which ascended the steepest incline in Belgrade. Several months pregnant, an injured woman sat huddled in the doorway to his mother's apartment building, her eyes averted from his own. Apparently she could walk no further unassisted. Her legs were curled up under her buttocks. Menninger paused to look at her. She assumed he was wondering if there was something he could do. When he went to bend to take a closer look, she spat directly in his face. Before he could react to this, a gang of street youth carrying clubs turned a corner and were coming his way. He flattened himself against the front of the building in order to let them pass.

\*

"What is occurring? Do you understand this, Albert? How could they do this, Albert?"

"Come away from the window, mother. You can only upset yourself."

She said, "They were beating people. Even women. For no reason." Like a child, Menninger's mother put her hands to her ears.

"You know how the military is, dear. They love to make noise. Try not to listen. Besides, remember, they'll tire of this sooner or later. We'll just have to do our best, okay?"

"What are they doing, Albert?"

"Things will soon be back to normal," he assured her. "Milosevic's men are rattling their sabers. So are the students."

"That's all it is?"

"That's all it is, they're rattling their sabers at each other, so we'll all do just what they say. The students have thrown in with the nationalists. They're trying to establish themselves as an insurmountable force."

His mother shook her head. "I don't understand," she told him.

"The SPO is being deliberately provocative," he explained.

"So are the students," she countered. "Each wants to be the occupying force here. The government is trying to keep us in line. I just don't understand it."

"Milosevic needs to diminish our will to resist him and his thugs. Not just the undergraduates and the SPO, not just the idealists, but all of Belgrade."

His mother asked, "How long will they be doing this, Albert?"

He answered, "For a while, I imagine. Don't worry. All they want to do is to frighten us. They don't mean us any harm. Not if we stay out of the streets. Who are we to them, right? We're not the enemy, we're small potatoes."

"You won't go out. You won't leave," his mother pleaded.

A flew blocks away from the Cardiological Institute where he was enrolled as a medical student, not far from the crumbling student dormitories, he had taken a shortcut across the outer edge of the university campus in order to get to the street. Coming from the other direction was a middle-aged man in a Chesterfield. He identified himself as a plainclothes policeman and said Menninger was under arrest for subversive activity. Who had turned him in — or why — was anyone's guess, but there wasn't time to think about that at the moment; Menninger began to backpedal, as if he were on a football field, in the middle of a scrimmage. Then, from over Menninger's shoulder, came a deafening roar. The next thing Menninger knew, a government tank was barreling past him.

At the sight of the oncoming tank, an expression of surprise registered on the officer's face. He had time to get out of its path, and it was not as though he didn't recognize the tank for what it was, it was a military tank, clearly coming in his direction, rather it was as though the officer couldn't imagine why the tank was not in the street, where it belonged: The street was the place for oncoming traffic. Menninger had a similar thought himself. He wondered what a military tank thought it was doing in the carefully manicured green of the medical fellows' garden.

The next thing he knew, the tank had sheared the policeman in half. It didn't leave the man mangled, or particularly bloody for that matter — divided, was all, a torso neatly severed from its lower extremities.

"No, of course not. Where were you this afternoon, mother? I tried to phone here once I heard on the radio Milosevic was sending in his troops. At first the telephone rang with no answer, then the lines went dead entirely."

"This was my musical afternoon," she said. "Don't you remember what day of the week it is?"

"Oh yes, of course. Where was it today?" Menninger asked.

"Matthias Church," his mother responded. She held out a crumpled paper quarto. He straightened it. He stood beside a chair and read what it said. The paper was a musical program with a line drawing of a violin, or perhaps a cello, in the center of its cover.

Each week at this time his mother and a few of her lady friends attended a chamber recital of some sort, then retired to the Café Gerbeaud where they gossiped over sherry.

"Let's close the curtains," said Menninger. "Would you like me to do that, dear? Would you like me to close the curtains?"

"No, but turn on electric lamps all the same. It will soon be rather dark in here — No?"

"All right, dear," Menninger answered, pulling the curtains together. "We'll turn on a lamp or two, if that's what you like."

Menninger's mother said, "Did you speak to the doorman about that man, Albert?"

"What man, mother?"

"The one I asked you to see to — who else? That hobo who lurks about and begs money when I pass him. You didn't forget, did you?"

Menninger lied, "No mother, I didn't forget." Menninger's mother had pointed out a Muslim who'd begun loitering around their building. He was tall and thin wearing a turtleneck sweater beneath an old tunic. Instead of trousers, he wore plus-fours that were several sizes too big for him and fell well below the knee. He appeared to Menninger to be blind. He wore sunglasses with round, black lenses and carried a white cane. But he wasn't blind, as Menninger's mother pointed out. When he thought no one was watching, he changed his shaky gait to a long, confident stride, and did without the cane entirely.

"And?"

"And Alia said he'd see about it, mother. He's had several complaints, I understand. I wouldn't be too worried though. He's surely just an old man, down on his luck."

"Does that give him the right to make a nuisance of himself? Is that what you're saying? Then I think the opposite. No, it does not. He has no business being there. Let him go back to where he came from."

Menninger sat down in a chair and began emptying his pockets of his wallet and keys. Without looking up, Menninger asked, "How was your recital mother? I don't believe you've said."

"Oh, very bad."

"Really? Inferior musicians? That's unusual, isn't it?"

"Not the organist, Albert. With her I had no complaint. Very expert."

"What then, the music they selected?"

"No, the program was fine as well. But the afternoon wasn't pleasant. You never know who you'll be sitting next to anymore. My generation was brought up to regard music with a proper respect. Not everyone seems to feel that today. Audiences are often very rude, very restless."

"Perhaps they thought there was something wrong with the playing," Menninger suggested.

"Even when they like a work, they show their pleasure coarsely. That ruins it for everyone."

"Perhaps you should skip a week or two. Have your friends over here, why don't you, mother? Would you consider that?"

How could Belgrade, the Serbian capital, allow harm to come to any of its most learned and cultured citizens? That's what she was thinking, wasn't it? No wonder she demanded to live on the Nsykli Hill overlooking the Sava. Nsykli was a hill, a towering limestone mesa, while Belgrade itself was a lowland, repeatedly razed to the ground then rebuilt through much of its early history. Her apartment was on Mihaly-Tancsics Street in a fine old baroque building, the Erdoly-Palais. From the window of her front room, in one direction you could see a prayer house that dated back to the fifteenth century, and in the other direction, past the shattered minarets of a prominent mosque, modern Belgrade and the lights along the river. She described her home to others as "looking out over the city," but the truth was, thought Menninger, the apartment looked down on it, particularly on what went on in its streets and its ghettos. On his mother's side of the Sava, a person of culture and means could rise above such things.

No doubt she felt like a Serb, completely at home here in Belgrade, the Serbian capital. What was the time-worn expression, "Speak Serbian so the world can understand you?" But they weren't Serbs at all, not as Milosevic was defining things. While she'd lived here all of her life, her parents had been from Dubrovnik, in the neighboring republic of Croatia, and their parents before them. Right now it was Muslims who were being ousted from their apartments and taken to the ghettos of Belgrade, but there was no guarantee it would stop there. Already anyone of Croatian blood was having trouble getting visas, while no Muslim could travel at all. Twice he'd encouraged her to leave the city. Twice she'd said no. This, after all, was her home. She'd seen armies in the street before, and she'd seen governments come and go. To his mother, Milosevic was just another shady politician.

"But if people stop attending, won't they end these series entirely?" she asked him.

"What, dear? What did you say? Look, the conditions in Belgrade are very bad. I don't have any way of knowing how long there'll be concerts. Surely you realize that."

"I just feel one should do what one can, Albert. By way of support."

Menninger rubbed at his eyes with his fingers. He felt a headache coming on — a large round ball that was lodging itself directly behind the bridge of his nose. He said, "Who do you think you're supporting, mother? Bach?

Liszt? Mendelssohn?"

"Mendelssohn is no longer played," she reported. "Strictly forbidden."

"I know, I know, another of the government's master strokes. Nothing by a Jew. But that's not the point, dear."

"Perhaps we should talk about something else, if this upsets you, Albert."

"Well it does seem a little obscene. Doesn't it seem that way to you, mother? I mean, there are people down on the streets collecting twigs and sticks. They've been put out of their homes. You see, they don't know where they'll be sleeping tonight. The conditions in Belgrade are really very bad, dear."

"Oh, very bad. Yes, there's so much unemployment. And distress everywhere," his mother said. "Do you think I'm blind to that? Do you think I'm unaware of the moral depravity? I see people who have lost their last scrap of dignity."

His nerves felt raw. Menninger said, "It must seem a little obscene, then, even to you, to concern yourself with an organ recital."

She asked, "Would it improve them one iota if we spoke of something else? I don't see how, do you?"

"I'm simply suggesting that what's vicious and tawdry, what's criminal, mother, may spring from hunger and from poverty, and most of all, from fear."

"Really, Albert? How would you know? You received the best schooling, here and abroad. When have you been hungry? Can you remember a time when I allowed you to be cold? Was there a way to spoil you which I wouldn't allow?"

"I apologize, mother. I didn't mean to lecture you."

Menninger went to the window and saw not the Sava at the moment but billowing clouds of blackness through a parting in the curtains. He was surprised when he turned to find his mother at his shoulder. She'd come for more reassurance.

"There's no reason to be afraid, dear, at least not as long as we keep out of their way. They won't stay very long, the army. If they overcome the SPO and these others, they'll leave an occupying force behind, little more than a handful of soldiers, while the bulk of their troops push out to the provinces. We'll simply have to be patient. And cautious, of course. Why don't you take a hot tub, dear? Would you like me to draw your bath and bring you something sweet to drink?"

"Yes, I'll take a hot tub, I think, Albert."

"Should I draw it for you then?"

"No, no. I'll do it myself."

"Are you certain? I don't mind."

"Would you like a little nibble first? I might. Are you hungry?"

"No. Not at all."

His mother said, "All that lives must die. Passing through nature to eternity."

Menninger said, "No Shakespeare, mother. Not just now. Please. *Hamlet* has nothing to teach us about what's happening in the streets."

His mother paused in the dining room on her way to her closets. She was watching him, or facing at least in his general direction. She removed a hanky from her sleeve. Curiously, he thought, she brought her hanky to her mouth instead of to her cheeks, the way other women seemed to. She might have been bringing a napkin to her lips. She said, "You were always a cold fish, even as a child." There was nothing critical in his mother's tone. She seemed to be articulating a judgment she had long ago reached but never before found occasion to voice. It was possible she had not intended for him to hear at all. Nevertheless, he heard, felt stung, and he answered her in kind.

"I'm not sure I know what that means, mother. What, precisely, is a cold fish?"

"Look in the mirror," she answered.

They stood facing one another. She waited for him to respond. When he failed to, she walked away.

He returned his attention to the window. If the students began a retreat, the first thing the soldiers would destroy would be — what? The main bridge? Yes, the Bridge of Brotherhood and Unity, he imagined. Then the ones that remained. They would push them back to the part of Belgrade commonly known as Student City. In the distance, he could hear what sounded like rockets and mortar fire, though that seemed out of the question. Everything was suddenly silent outside. He waited for the breaking of the silence, virtually holding his breath. At last he heard a drilling noise, human voices, other kinds of noise which he couldn't identify, but human noise, crazed laughter, perhaps, then, finally, a few rounds of rifle fire, at once defiant and pathetic.

In a few minutes, he heard a knock at their door which interrupted such concentration. He told his mother not to answer it. She called from the kitchen, "I won't become a prisoner in my own home, Albert, the thought is completely absurd." Before he could move from the window to stop her, she was speaking to a pair of government officials who asked if they might step inside. She seemed surprised to learn they were looking for her son, the way one is always surprised by the casual incompetence of any poorly salaried bureaucrat, the way one's surprised when they are formal and polite.

That was her thought as well as she watched from the window as the larger of the two officials touched the crown of Albert's head as they put him in the back seat of their car, for fear Albert might injure himself. She'd been about to prepare her favorite snack, cream of tomato soup, a cup of orange Pekoe tea. She'd meant to take it to her room on a tray she had purchased while traveling to the Orient with his father when her son was only a child, a red lacquered tray with parasols stenciled in gold, and now, about to return to the kitchen so she might finish what she'd started, she wondered to herself how the government could possibly make this up to her.

# PART TWO

# Wollicott's Traveling Rabbit's Foot Minstrels

## I.

*In Which The Wollicotts Prepare For Divorce, Sally And Powell*

Sally Wollicott drops by. She's wearing a denim skirt, a white linen camp shirt, and a pair of hightop Reeboks. She looks lighter and freer than she's ever looked before. She's come to tell me about Richard, her lover. She's been seeing Richard on the side during the last few months of her marriage to Powell and now Richard wants them to move in together. That is, he wants to move in with Sally and the kids.

That's what she's come by to tell me: about Richard, my Ex. Her lover. The man who wants to move in with Sally and the kids. Once her husband Powell moves out.

"I knew you wanted out of the marriage — but Sally, for Richard?"

"I didn't know how to tell you, Cassie," Sally continues.

"You seem to be doing all right."

"If you found out it was Richard, I thought you might be hurt."

"Betrayed is more like it."

"Look," Sally says, "if you put your car up for sale on consignment, and if I started looking at the car, and if I found out whose it was, I'd tell you, right?"

She says this with such earnestness that both of us break out laughing. "God," Sally says. "Can you believe we're having this conversation?"

"I didn't know you even knew him," I say.

"I didn't. I mean I see him on TV. Well, very casually."

"Well, so — so that's good," I say. "So — you're in love with Richard now. That's good."

"Come on," Sally says. "Who do you know who's in love anymore?"

This was several months ago, the better part of a year by now. Now, as for Richard: who he is, where he fits into my life.

Richard is a television weather man. I meet Richard at a party. I've just broken up with this lunatic in Manhattan and caught the first plane for Phoenix. Richard's just broken up with a figure skater. I marry him.

We move to Paradise Valley. Half a year later, I'm standing at the foot of the driveway, watering our lawn. Richard's in the Toyota. He has his right hand on the headrest of the passenger seat, his right arm extended, his chin on his shoulder. This is a moment I remember quite clearly. It's the moment I see that he means to run me down. For a split second I see the whole incident about to happen in his eyes. I see not only my death, but that he has been planning this for months, that he's thought it through. I see not only the neighbors coming out of their houses and Richard bending over me. I don't just see myself looking up into his eyes. I see what Richard sees as well. I see myself looking like so much run over fruit that's been left on the watery pavement.

As we're working out the settlement, he trades in the Toyota as an act of good faith. "You tried to run me over. It wasn't the car," I say. "It was you. I'd think you'd be on to yourself by now. You're a maniac, Richard. A psychopath."

Then later. Working out our settlement.

Fred, Richard's Attorney: "Did he kick you, Cassie?"

Me: "No."

"Did he tie you up?"

"No, not once."

"Did he punch you in the kidneys, hold you under a scalding shower, lock you in the trunk of a car?"

Barry, my attorney: "Look, Fred, this isn't getting us anywhere. What's your point?"

What sort of question is that? I know what his point is: I can make you look foolish. I can make you look neurotic, like a two-tone purple bitch. Think about it, Cassandra, do you really want to go toe to toe with me in a court of law?

Richard, I think, Richard you poor thing, you should have hired yourself a woman. This guy doesn't have any more idea of who I am than you do.

Fred says, "I'm just trying to see what we can agree on and what we can't. It seems to me, it seems to us, actually, that Cassie's asking for a great deal of money."

Now, Fred to me again: "Isn't it true that you're plagued by irrational fears?"

"No."

"Do you fear heights, the air? Do you dream of death by drowning?"

"Not once, no. Never."

"Do you have an ongoing interest in infection?"

"No," I answer.

"How many bacteria are there in a sneeze?"

"Do I have to answer that?" I ask Barry.

"I don't see why not — if you know the answer."

I look to Barry, hoping he's enjoying this as much as I am, but he seems too stunned by the question to be aware of such things. Well, I'm enjoying it, anyway. Three men in the same room hanging on to my every word.

I move in with my attorney. Barry, my attorney, becomes Richard's casual friend. Barry will admit this, but only once Barry marries me, and reluctantly even then. They don't drink together, they don't socialize. Paradise Valley is the toniest part of Scottsdale, a world unto itself, a village, says Barry. A couple who divorce have roots in a community that have nothing to do with their marriage. They have jobs, friends, mortgages to pay on, memberships in clubs. What are they suppose to do, steal off into the night? You're just being theatrical, Cassie. For God's sake —

"Decide where your loyalties lie, Barry," I say. "The man tried to kill me. That would seem to count for something. Why do you make me feel as though I'm intruding on your rights? What could you find to talk to him about?"

"What does anyone find to talk about?" he says. "We speak to one another. You know, Hello, how are you? What about this weather! What about those Suns! We run into each other, you realize."

"I'd think you'd feel funny."

"I do. But I'd feel funnier trying to ignore him."

"That's great," I say. "That's rich. How would you feel if I was in league with your enemies?"

"Is that what you think? We're ganging up against you now?"

Richard, in brief.

## II.

*In Which The Hearrons Prepare For Their Party*

Sally is getting a divorce from Powell. That's where the story began. I'm married to Barry. Barry Hearron. Barry and Powell are law partners. They're the founders of the law firm, Wollicott and Hearron and Blah Blah Blah Blah Blah. Also, Barry and Powell are equal partners in a hot air balloon they fly on the weekends. They fly it in full regalia, helmets and jodhpurs and boots, and silk blouses a woman would die for.

To ease Powell's pain from a messy separation, they decide to spend money. Barry puts the balloon up for sale. The Rabbit's Foot, the first balloon, gets sold on a Tuesday. The Finest, the second, the one they've had their eye on, they buy within the week. As near as I can tell, it's bigger, faster, younger, blonder. The finest. They buy it. To celebrate its purchase, they decide to throw a party and invite all of their clients. Tonight we're having that party.

That brings us to this morning. That is, the morning of the night of the party. It's a Sunday morning and Sally is standing in my living room, a child in each arm, Jami in the right one, Alicia in the left — two little birds in the arms of a biped.

Sally and Richard are calling it quits. "What happened?" I ask. Did they have a fight? Did he beat her up? Did he hit her? Kick her? Punch her in the kidneys? Hold her under a scalding shower? Lock her in the trunk of a car?

"No, nothing like that," Sally answers. They just don't seem to be having any fun anymore.

"I wonder what it's going to be like?" she says to herself.

"Tonight, I mean. Embarrassing, I'm sure. I mean at the party, Richard, Powell, and me. The three of us together under the same roof, at the same time."

She tells the kids to play outside, then she goes to the CD player and puts on the Stones, "Jumpin' Jack Flash," then heads for the liquor. "Aperitif, Cassie?"

Sally pours half an of inch of liquor into each glass, looks them over, thinks better of it, and pours another two inches. "Sally," I say, "it's ten o'clock in the morning."

She hands me mine. "This is the adult dosage, Cass," she answers. "To the Minstrels." This is Sally's old name for us: Wollicott's Traveling Rabbit's Foot Minstrels.

### III.

*In Which Barry Shares A Confidence With His Wife, Cassie*

Barry's below in the yard. Sally's just left. I'm sitting in our bedroom window. "What's next?" I ask him.

"Where's the Rego valve?"

I point to something, taking a chance, and Barry says, "That? No, that's the spit tube."

"Right. How'bout over there?" I say, gesturing with my glass.

"No, Cassie, no way. It ought to be right about — here," Barry says.

I say to him, "Did you ever think about calling it The Trial Balloon?"

"What?"

"You could change its name. Instead of calling it The Finest, you could call it The Trial Balloon."

"The Trial Balloon?" Barry asks.

"A little joke."

"Right."

"You and Powell being lawyers, I mean."

"No, I get it, Cassie. All I'm asking is that you try it and see for yourself. Look, why don't you start with the basket. No envelope, no propane, no nothing. We won't even start up the burner. Just climb into the basket and try to get a feel for it."

The burner that produces the heat to keep the thing aloft is reduced to a series of valves and plumbing. Barry has this all laid out across a series of newspapers on the patio. The point is to get it back together before the caterers come. This is something the caterers thought up, to tether the balloon in the middle of everything. This is what I get for leaving Barry on his own, caterer-wise.

It looks to me now as though we're about to have the largest centerpiece in catering history, which, if it doesn't bother Barry, doesn't really bother me, and will probably make the caterer famous. The basket sits near the barbecue. Off to one side of the yard, the deflated balloon has been stretched and smoothed; but since it's bigger than the space it occupies, it is curved around. An accommodation to our hurricane fencing.

"I'm afraid of heights."

Barry says, "You're leaning out of a second story window, you realize. From where you are right now, you could fall and break your neck."

"Is that suppose to be an inducement?"

"I'm just saying that everything is relative. Sometimes the dangers you perceive are nothing in comparison to the ones you overlook."

No guts, no glory — is that it, Barry? I thought women were suppose to be the ones with hormones. What's gotten into you? I think you ought to see a doctor, I really do, I think you've got a case of the MALES this morning. You're dangerously close to a testosterone frenzy.

"It is possible to be happy, Cassandra, that's all I'm saying."

"Tell me, Barry: Are we having a fight?"

"We're not having anything. I'm just saying that it wouldn't be a bad idea to give it a try."

"On what grounds?"

"What?"

"What makes trusting your life to some colored cloth and a little wicker basket anything other than a bad idea?"

"Because you might have some fun. You might enjoy it."

"You've got to do better than that," I tell him.

"It's like falling in love," Barry tells me. "A time when anything is possible. Do you know what I mean?"

I know what he means. He means the time when you think, This could be great. This could change everything.

"Take anything else," he goes on, "and I'm fixed, you know? Productively compulsive, Cassie. But this —"

"This is bigger than the both of us?" Barry's moments of introspection are so few and far between that I feel guilty for making fun of him, so, without missing a beat, I say, "I wouldn't say you're fixed, exactly. You just see things in rather solid terms."

"Right. But in a balloon, see — All right, Cassandra, what is it *you* want out of life?"

Barry looks up at me in the second story window. He puts his hand in front of his face to shield his eyes from the sun and says, "What's that you've got in your hand?"

I look at it myself, this glass of yellow Cointreau, then hold it up as if I'm toasting Sally. "Sally," I say. "Remember?"

"Right, Sally," Barry says, shaking his head. "Do you know what time it is?"

"It's still morning, I think."

"Right, well. Just don't forget about the party tonight, Cassie. It might be nice to start it sober."

"You were telling me about Richard, Barry. Tell me again why Richard's been invited."

"I don't see why that should be awkward. And besides, Cassie, he's a client now. It's not like I singled him out, or tried to make a point of it. I don't see why you're embarrassed. All the clients were invited. What did you expect me to do, leave his name off the list?"

Here's what you've missed since I interrupted Barry: I've been telling him what Sally told me. Sally told me that Barry and Powell had taken Richard on as a client. According to Sally, here's the way that happened. Barry met Richard at a bar called Aunt Chilada's. Richard had come from a squash match, and one thing led to another. They began talking business. Richard and a few of his friends are forming a Master Limited Partnership and opening a restaurant. Over an icy banana daiquiri, Richard retained Barry to represent him in this. That's pretty much the gist of it.

Now I say to Barry, "What does Richard know about running restaurants? I lived with the man. I know the way his mind works. He thinks the four basic food groups are Instant, Take-Out, There On The Table When I Get Home, and Häagen-Dazs."

"He won't be running it. Someone else will. Did you pick up the dry cleaning?"

"It's hanging in your closet. What sort of restaurant is it, did he say?"

"He might have. Who knows? What difference does it make? We're talking tax shelters, Cassie, not a career in a cuisine. Why this sudden burst of curiosity about what I do at the firm?"

"It's not you we're talking about, Barry. It's Richard. You remember Richard. My Ex? Why do I have to hear that you've taken him on as a client from Sally? Don't you think it might have been better to tell me yourself?"

"You're making too much out of this. It's got nothing to do with you. It's business. A little paper work, an hour or two in a meeting. It's no big deal, Cassie, believe me."

"This doesn't have anything to do with him breaking up with Sally does it?"

"I didn't know he was. Breaking up with Sally."

"Richard's not. Not to hear her tell it. She's breaking up with him."

"What's wrong," Barry asks, "aren't they having any fun anymore?"

\*

Mid-afternoon, the caterers arrive. They arrive in matching panel trucks and begin setting up tables all over our property. They set out crates of plastic glasses that look as though they're crystal, then crystal glasses and fine china plates. I help them get started. A man in charge introduces himself, then later introduces himself again. I don't quite catch his name either time. A bit later, I open all of our doors to them, and it isn't long before they seem to be the ones who belong in this house and I seem to be an intruder.

The house seems filled with important activity, and it's nice to be apart from that. It's nice to hear footsteps on the stairs and voices on the lawn and to know that someone, anyone, is putting out the paraphernalia that you need to have fun, and all the rest of us will have to do is to try to be gracious. If that sounds cynical, it should sound only drunk, for I've been sipping liquor since speaking with Sally.

The more I drink, the more I enjoy the thought of the caterers. They take those small, neurotic steps that make them appear to be wearing straight skirts, the men as well as the women, and I watch them from my window, for I'm hiding upstairs. I watch them ignoring Barry and all of Barry's friends. They're in a huff about Barry, and this group of his balloon friends. I pick out two, Powell and Barry, who are staring down at the ground, their hands on their hips. Deflated, the balloon looks sad, expansive, terrestrial. What are the chances they'll have it ready in time? It makes me feel sorry for the pair of them, though that may be the liquor.

Twice, Maurice — Morris? — has come to my bedroom door, shaken his head, and said, "This really won't do."

I've shaken my head too, and then Maurice — Morris? — has left me alone.

Finally, late afternoon, Barry comes upstairs. He says, "Here you are, Cassie."

I say, "Tell me again, who have we invited?"

"I told you, our clients, some friends."

"All the right people?"

"What's that suppose to mean?"

"Oh, you know. Powerful men and their smartly dressed wives."

"That's right, Cassie. And their well-appointed cars.

You're very drunk, you realize?"

Barry's right about this. I mean, he's right that I'm drunk, but I'll be sober by the time the party begins, and, anyway, that's not really his point. His point has to do with his values. Who am I to be so smug? Why do I like to make ambition sound cheap? Who am I to be so judgmental? There won't be anyone here at our house tonight that I'd be unwilling to meet if we saw them in a restaurant. There won't be anyone whose house I'd refuse to be a guest in. There won't be anyone here I'd be ashamed to introduce to any of our friends.

I'm twenty-seven years old, I've never held an adult job, and the truth is, if it wasn't for Barry, the only way I could get into a house like this is with a tray of shrimp in my hands. And not once, not once in all the time we've been married, has he ever brought that up to me.

"Why the long face, Cassie?" Barry asks me. "What's gotten into you? I don't know what you want anymore. Tell me. What can I do?"

"What can you do?"

"That's it."

"See to it that I never have to try on another bathing suit?"

Barry rolls his eyes toward the ceiling. "Barry," I continue, "do you think Sally's deeply, importantly attractive, or do you think she's simply superficially attractive?"

"I think you're drunk, Cassie. And I think we have guests coming."

At some point, Barry, I may sober up, so there's something I want to tell you before I lose the thought. Has it ever occurred to you that men and women are different? I'm serious. That's why there's so much trouble between husbands and wives — I mean, that's a possibility, isn't it? Take us. Take you. Take this house. The house is yours, ours, a matter of ownership between a husband and wife. Well, that's not what it is to me. It's a nest. It's this nest I make that you come to and live in. I go out into the world and bring back bits of tinfoil and cellophane wrappers. Is this making any sense? I spend my life creating activities for the two of us that are safe enough to share, dinners, weekends away, moments alone. Would it have to be you that I shared them with? Which is more important, that I share them with you, or simply that I share them with someone familiar? Why, when there are hooks in this nest, do I just assume you put them there?

"Can I tell you something?" Barry asks me. "It looks to me as though Powell's thinking twice about the divorce. It's nothing he's said, exactly. But he seems to be dragging his feet." Barry shakes his head. He means to leave the impression of a tragic mistake. "I was glad when he walked out on her. That's a mean-hearted thing to say, I suppose, but it's true. I thought that was best all around. Well, relieved."

"Why's that?"

"I just thought it would be better if she were out of his life. And out of our lives, actually."

"What's wrong with Sally?"

"Personally, I don't have much feeling for her one way or the other. It's you I'm thinking about."

"What about me, Barry? Spit it out. What are you trying to say?"

"Well, I mean it's so obvious that she hates you."

"Sally," I say, trying to be sure I'm following him.

"It's more complicated than that. She's jealous of you as

well, I suppose. And envious. And God-knows-what-all. Psychologically, the woman's a mess. In some dark, murky way, she may even be fond of you. But the hatred that woman feels for you, Cassandra — It's palpable when you're in the same room. It's just so obvious that it makes people uncomfortable. I know it makes me uncomfortable; maybe me most of all."

"Sally Wollicott, Barry? My best friend in the world?"

Barry looks at me as though I'm being deliberately difficult, or coy, neither of which he has patience for. "Think back. Think of all the things Sally's done over the years to try to sabotage you. Look at yourself right now, for God's sakes. She knows we're having this party. She came over here and got you drunk. And she had to get up early to do it. It's probably been the first time that woman's been out of bed before noon in the last fifteen years."

"No one got me drunk, Barry. For better or worse, I've gotten drunk on my own."

"That's my point. That's what she senses. These antennae of hers go up whenever the two of you are together, and she just can't leave you alone."

"Thank you for sharing this with me, Barry."

"Well, wouldn't you say you're a tad on the self-destructive side. I mean, just look at you."

Barry's getting ready to shower. He puts his robe over his shoulder and starts for the bathroom. I say, "If this is so important, I mean, if you're so sure you're right about this, why haven't you brought it up before now?"

This stops him in his tracks. He looks puzzled, dazed. "I thought it might embarrass you, why else?"

## IV.

*In Which The Hearrons Throw A Party In Honor Of All That Is BiggerFasterYoungerBlonder*

Our guests fill the house, and behind the house, on our property, the balloon fills the night like some drowsy, gentle giant. I'm sober by this point, or sober enough. Powell comes late and Barry lets him in. I brace myself to face Sally with Richard, but when I see Sally it's only in passing, and she's all by herself. I'm chatting up a group of Barry's favored clients. Sally takes my hand as she passes, and then the two of us embrace. This gives her a chance to whisper in my ear, "He's put you with the heavy-hitters, huh? Don't be nervous. It's going to be lovely."

"Where's Richard?" I whisper back.

"Who knows? I came alone. Richard's date is right over there."

"Her? You're not serious."

"Straight out of the cast of 'The Road Warrior.' Do you believe it?"

"When did this happen? Has Richard moved out? Already?"

"How can he? He sublet his house. I told him he couldn't bring her home, not with Jami and Alicia around. I told him if he was going to sleep with her, they'd have to go back to her place. Do you think that's unreasonable?"

"That's not unreasonable," I say.

"Cheers," Sally says, showing me her glass.

After I've made a round or two of the room, I go upstairs to the bathroom off the master bedroom and use it, then run water on my face. I decide to re-do my make-up. I dry my hands and decide to put on my make-up at the vanity table, but when I come out of the bathroom, it's already taken. Richard's date, who Sally's pointed out of me, is leaning toward the mirror, reapplying her mascara. Her hair's dyed black, cut butch, and her clothes are fashionably preposterous. She's young, I see, now that I can see her up close, but she's poised too, and French. How do I know this? I haven't heard her speak, and if I see it now, why didn't I see it before, when I first saw her downstairs, a stand-out, beacon of a girl in a room full of women, all of them moisturized and creamed, all tailored or hatted and booted? I sit on the edge of our bed, looking over her shoulder.

She is young enough, or French enough, to feel oblivious to me, and I find this — don't ask me why, it is *my* house, after all, my vanity — I find this endearing. Finally she sees me in the mirror and speaks.

"You're Cassie, yes? Cassandra?"

"And you're?"

"Chloe," she says.

"Chloe," I repeat.

"Please?"

"Your name. It's beautiful."

"Yes? Thank you for inviting me," she continues. "Your house. It's precisely — *appointed*. Heavily weighted?" She senses that she's lost something from French to English, like a few cents she might have lost in a rate of exchange, then she says, "I hope not to make you uncomfortable."

"Because of Richard?"

"Yes, Richard."

"How is Richard? I haven't seen him yet."

"I think he means to try to avoid you. Men can be like

little boys, yes? Quite like children."

She puts a few things away in her clutch, then comes to the bed where I'm sitting. She stares at me as though I'm the foreigner in this conversation, then says. "Cassie — you are so...*unattached?*"

I shake my head no. No, that's not the word, probably.

"Self-contained?" Chloe says. But she brushes this away. She puts her arms around me and says (I think), "*C'est ne pas frequent que on trouve un person si acceptante que vous.*"

Barry comes to the bedroom door just as Chloe is going downstairs.

"Ah, here you are, Cassie," says Barry. He has a slight glow, as though he's had champagne, though it's a glow I know that has nothing to do with liquor. Barry is at home, in his element. He's at his best as a host.

"What was that all about?" he asks me.

"She's Richard's latest."

"I know. What was that she said to you?"

"I think she said I was a remarkable woman."

Barry grimaces. "You see? I mean, it's obvious, isn't it? Richard's told her all about Sally. It figures, doesn't it? How could she help but know how Sally feels toward you? I wish I had a way to make that woman vanish. I really do." Barry looks down at his hand, as if he'd like a magic wand, then says, "A magic wand or something."

\*

I pause at the foot of the stairs, and look around for Barry. Sitting on the lower stairs is a woman. She is balancing her cocktail glass in the palm of one hand, steadying it with the other, and this, and the fact that her hair's in a bun, gives me the impression of someone primly drinking tea, a woman I might see in the window of a sidewalk cafe having tea by herself. I don't want you to think I linger on this. I have my mind on other things. I only get a glimpse of her. She's a stranger to me, and judging from what she says, she doesn't know me either.

"Are these people friends of yours?" she says.

I'm still looking for Barry. I'm not thinking about what she probably has in mind — that the people she means are Barry and myself, the ones who are throwing the party, the couple whose house she is sitting in. "Some of them," I tell her.

"It's difficult to believe, isn't it? Just look at them. You know they don't act like this all the rest of the time. They have jobs, appointments. They live their lives in orderly fashion — except when they come to these parties."

The evening's still young. What can she be thinking of? Everyone's being pleasant. This woman's on the verge of unpleasantness, it's true, but even she's being orderly. What does she see that I've missed? What, about the party, seems disorderly, I wonder. I say to her, "Did you get anything to eat?"

She nods. "Be advised of the shrimp."

"You couldn't find anything?"

"Strictly standard issue."

"That's too bad. I'm sorry."

She takes a drink and looks at me, quizzically. "Why should you be sorry?"

"Because it's my party — ours, that is."

"I knew that," she says. "But, I mean, why should you be sorry?"

"Right," I say. "Good point. Excuse me."

Richard catches my eyes from across the room, then looks around, then looks down at his wrist as though he's late for an appointment. I look around too, then I make my way toward the back of the house. I go out through the sliding glass doors and take a long drink of my freshly-poured cocktail. I close my eyes in an attempt to appear to be catching my breath. When I open them, I see that Richard has done more or less the same thing. He's gone out through a side door, acted as if he wanted a moment to himself, then come around to the patio. The upshot of this is that we're standing shoulder to shoulder. Flight is in the air, but there's nowhere to flee to, which is what I'm reminded of when Richard says, "Good evening, Cassie. Are we speaking?"

"We're here. Do we have much choice, Richard?"

I can see our reflections in the glass. We are looking at the party progressing nicely behind the plate glass double doors. My house is spacious, beautifully decorated. The guests are pressing themselves up against one another. Someone's at the piano. The caterers are serving yet another round of something, which seems to find takers. Richard, in the reflected light, looks as feathery as always in the glass, and less prickly, less judgmental about the eyes and the corners of his mouth. I catch a glimpse of Barry on the other side of the room, still in his element, and I'm proud of him, quietly proud to be married to him. I'm glad that Richard can see me like this. I'm proud that I live in a nice house in a trendy neighborhood in a better part of the Sun Belt. It doesn't make me feel superficial. It makes me feel snug, and cared for. It makes me feel all the ways it's suppose to, I suppose, and that's fine, that's okay. It seems to me that everyone in-

side my house at this instant is well-kept, on their way, looking forward to something better, and it seems to me that
such things are too-easily undervalued.

Richard takes a sip of his drink and says, "What do you
think? Are they all uninteresting swine?"

"No. Not all of them."

"Chloe said she introduced herself to you."

"Yes, that's right. She did."

"I debated whether to bring her or not. I thought about
not coming myself, in fact, if you want to know the truth. I
wasn't sure which was worse, coming, as though we'd all
made up our minds to be adult about this, or staying away, as
though we'd decided to be honest with each other and go at
it from there."

"So you decided to come."

"Chloe decided, actually. She wanted to meet you, I
think."

I start to move to the other end of the patio. People are
trying to get through the doors at this end, in search of
some air. I take a few steps in the opposite direction, and
Richard, who I thought might be going back inside, falls into
step beside me. "She's very lovely," I say.

"That's for sure, Chloe is," Richard says. "Do you know
how I met her? The first time I saw her she was swimming
nude in a fish tank. She's a performance artist, I suppose
she told you. Sally and I and some friends were looking for
something to do. We were wandering around Hayden
Square. Near the university? We went up into this loft that
Sally had heard about. They were screening 'Splash.' Do
you remember that flick? The tank was in front of the
screen. All you could hear was this 16mm projector, since

the volume was turned off, and the sound of the compressor for the tank. I know how it sounds, silly, right? There were high school bleachers, not even any chairs. I was sitting on the bleachers beside Sally and I began to look around. People were straggling in late and acting like they were bored. They had their Westchester look on: Whatever this was, it wasn't art. How could it be art in Phoenix, Arizona? It was just some nude teenage girl swimming around in front of a screen where Tom Hanks was wooing Daryl Hannah. But after a few minutes you could see that they were into it. I mean, it was actually very sensuous, and you could tell that the men were looking at Chloe, desiring her, and that some of the women were feeling this too, or, whatever it is that women feel under those circumstances, maybe just a need to feel desired. And I looked at Chloe, and I thought to myself, `I'll bet that girl's a virgin. Or celibate, at least. No one but a person completely unaware of sex could possibly be so erotic.' And the truth is, she's both. What do you think about that?"

"I think you haven't changed, Richard."

"Really? That's nice to hear. That's good. That's such a nice thing to say to me, Cassie!"

We take a step or two toward the canopies, where the caterers are gathering up the empty chafing dishes and dinner services. The propane flame of Barry's hot air balloon has been left on just enough to keep the balloon filled out and aloft, and, in the spotlights, the caterers were right, I realize, for it has a kind of synthetic beauty. It's a little like seeing a whale. The balloon seems to be in proper proportion, and everything else seems in miniature. The balloon is multicolored, extra-terrestrial, and the tethers that keep it in place on the lawn look harmless. It looks like Gulliver among the Lilliputians, and the setting here is perfect for that, a landscape you could only come upon by chance. The property is floodlit and the lawn unfurls like a flag, ending in the distance at a reservoir, a water supply. There are boulders near the waterline to mark where our property ends and the state's begins anew, and the boulders, in the floodlight, seem white and other-worldly, as though they have fallen from some distant, ancient planet.

"So, Richard, what's this I hear about you becoming a restaurateur?"

"What?"

"Isn't that the story? I thought Sally said you'd spoken to Barry, or maybe it was Powell —to one of them, at any rate, about representing you. A restaurant?" I make eating motions with an imaginary fork, spearing food from my cocktail.

"Oh, that," Richard says. He seems amused by this. "Would you like to see my restaurant?" He sets our drinks on one of the serving tables. Before I can say anything, he takes me by the hand. He walks me to the balloon, then hoists himself up on the edge of the basket. He swings his legs around. There's an instrument panel on one side, and he reaches beneath it with his hand, searching blindly. At last he finds whatever he was reaching for. He extends his other hand to me. "Come on. Get in."

"Not on your life, Richard. What do you think you're doing?"

"Why don't you trust me Cassie?"

"Why don't I trust you, Richard? Look me in the eye. You tried to kill me. Do you suppose that could have something to do with it?"

"I can't believe you're still focusing on that."

"Do you deny that you wanted to kill me, Richard?"

Richard holds up a little plastic bag. He holds it between his thumb and first finger like it's a pair of someone's underpants, but then I see he's just being careful, that whatever it is, it's precious, apparently. I squint, shielding my eyes from the light from the flame and say, "Is that what I think it is?"

"That all depends, Cassie." He looks at me skeptically. "Don't tell me you don't know about this?"

"Is it Barry's?"

"It is as soon as he pays me for it."

Richard's perched on the padded trim of the basket; Richard still has his hand out to me. He says, "What do you think, should we sample some?"

Richard breaks the seal on Barry's stash of cocaine. I look toward the house. He puts a sample on his finger, then brings it to his tongue. Is it bitter, sweet, is it Barry's? How can it be Barry's? Why wouldn't I have known?

"I thought that was Barry's," I say.

"Half of it's yours. That's the law in this state, right?"

"Which half?" I ask, but Richard isn't listening. He licks the tip of his finger and says, "I don't think he'll mind, do you? It's a party. We're here to have fun."

"Don't you think it's a little breezy out tonight for this?"

"You're forgetting who you're dealing with here, Cassie. What do you say?"

Richard helps me into the basket and I watch as he lays down a line on an expensive Wedgwood mirror that he pulls from his jacket. With a precision that has always surprised me in Richard, he divides this. He rolls up a dollar bill, then, holding one nostril closed, he draws cocaine into the other. "What about it, Cassie?" he says, as though slightly out of breath.

I look down at the powder. I look back up at Richard. "I've been drinking all day," I say.

"Well?" says Richard.

"Well," I answer. It's been years since I've done a few lines of cocaine, and the thought of getting high in this particular way settles and rises, like the balloon overhead. I know what to expect. I'm not a novice at this. A cocaine rush makes me feel resolute. I feel as though I have perfect pitch when I'm high on cocaine, and that's how I want to feel at the moment, I realize, high and unfettered, a part of the night's festivities, unattuned to human failing.

I lean forward and take two lines of my own, which Richard has prepared wordlessly, breezelessly, despite a wind that's whipping up. I lean forward and draw up the lines and the rush is all it's suppose to be — immediate. I think that coke is one of the few things that's as good as you think it is going to be, and this makes me feel as though Richard isn't Richard, as if I'm younger and still beautiful and my life is still indivisible by petty crimes and bad mistakes. This lasts all of ten seconds. Then I feel miserable.

We lean back against the wicker. Richard looks at me. He says I look miserable.

"I feel miserable," I say.

"You really should tell Sally that. It would probably reassure her."

"Why is everyone talking to me about Sally tonight? Why is she on everyone's mind?"

"I wonder, Cassie."

"I'm serious."

"In a way, Cassie, you're the reason we're not together anymore, Sally and I. I suppose you realize that. It just got to be too much after a while. Well, you know her better than I do. Sally obsesses. She's obsessed with you. I mean, there's a very obsessive side to her, where you're concerned, and I got to the point where I just couldn't take it. It's like someone who has to wear khaki all the time. There's nothing wrong with khaki, but if you start to obsess about it, if you can't wear anything else, if you begin to schedule your weeks around the shades of khaki that you'll have to put on, then you're in a very unhealthy situation, actually. And that's not very pleasant to watch in someone you care about."

"What?"

"Nothing," Richard says.

"Richard, can you tell me the truth about something?"

"I can try."

"Barry says that Sally hates me."

Richard shakes his head. "I don't think so. Not really. She just wants to do you harm. In some odd way, in fact, I think she may love you. She may love you more, in fact, than she's ever loved a man. Why else would you have this effect on her? I never had any effect on her. You know Powell and Sally, you tell me: did Powell have any particular effect on her?"

"I resent that. You make it sound as though I'm the one responsible for this, that I've driven her to do these things."

"Whoa! Hold your horses. What things? Just what are the charges here? Be specific, Cassie. What do you think she's done to you?"

I have to stop and think. Richard continues, "I mean, let's

face it, it's not what she's done. What matters is that you can't trust her. And you can't really hold her responsible for that. It's not as if she sat down one day and decided to betray you. It's not as if she willed herself to feel this way about you, Cassie."

"I don't know," I say. I start to get up, then think better of it. Richard watches this, doubtfully. I'm aware of Richard watching, aware that he doubts I'm in command of my faculties. It is a look on Richard's face that I have seen before, an opinion he maintains that my life is less substantial than his own. When we were married, this look came over his face whenever he was deciding to kiss me, and I wonder if he's going to try that now, here, in my own backyard, with my house within shouting distance. And I wonder if I'll be more relieved if he does, in which case I'll stop him — or if he doesn't, which will leave me wondering why. "Sit down," Richard says.

I do.

"Can you walk?" Richard asks me.

"I doubt it."

"You need to go inside," Richard says. "You'll be missed."

Richard lays down two more lines. He takes one and offers the second to me. I take it. That's pretty much the order of things. Then we sit there, saying nothing. For how long, I don't know. Finally I say something, or Richard does, but in any case, it's Richard who asks a question.

Richards asks, "What's that?"

There are birds not far from our property. Barry says that they're loons that have built their nests at the reservoir, but he knows I can't tell one bird from any other, and this may be a way of refusing to answer, or maybe a joke. Maybe there are no loons in the desert. In any case, there are birds of some kind, making some kind of bird-sound, and Richard is feeling the first shrill effects of a cocaine paranoia, as familiar as a guard at a gate. "Loons," I say. "You know, Richard — I think the worst part. I mean, the very worst part — It just makes me feel like a fool. Who would have thought she was jealous of me?"

"You sound as though you're embarrassed. Don't be so hard on yourself," Richard says to me. "No one understands the effect they have on anyone else. And it's probably just as well. We'd probably just give up. I mean, we might do something foolish if we ever got a grasp on things."

"That's a pose, Richard. Now you're just taking a position."

"Take a deep breath, Cassie," Richard says. "What do you smell?"

I take a deep breath and say, "Cooked food. Those little cans of Sterno. Someone's smoking hash, I think. Wet grass. The night."

"You're missing it. It's the desert. When the winds are right, there's a ceiling inversion. It's called the Transcontinental. It's the one thing meteorological thing I know about." He takes another breath.

"That's the blow, Richard."

"It's great, isn't it?" Richard stands up in the basket and stretches. "I mean, sometimes it's the only thing that keeps me going."

Richard straddles the basket, gets out, leaves me sitting. He takes a few unsteady steps, then rights himself and sets off for the house. Unexpectedly, he stops. He turns to me and says, "Oh, Cassie. There's one more thing you should know." I brace myself for this, ready for anything. Richard says, "No one calls it *blow* anymore."

\*

Sitting in the basket by myself is a little like sitting in a row boat. I mean the moment you get in and discover that it's leakless. You find it sets well in the water, that it carries your weight, that it is tight as a drum. It is not like sitting in a row boat at all, of course, since there's a flame overhead, and beyond the flame, the rich dark hues of the fabric. But in some ways it is reminiscent of being set afloat from a safe wooded shore, a familiar shore where you own a summer home, and I am high enough on liquor and cocaine to feel sure of myself, and as worthy of the water as the row boat itself. I am not, in other words, startled by Barry's call, "Cassandra? Are you out here? Where are you, Cassandra? Come on, Cassandra, what's become of you?" That, I think, is a very good question, if not a particularly startling one, and under other circumstances, one I'd like to discuss.

"Cassie," Barry calls. "Come on now."

Is it me that's lost, or you, Barry? I can't tell from your voice. Speak up. Speak more clearly. There's too much talk as a rule, from too many corners, but tonight, just this once, I can hear your voice — it's a beacon — and I will follow it home, if you'll give me the chance. Enunciate. Articulate, Barry.

"Cassandra, this isn't funny now. Are you out here in the dark?"

"I'm here," I call.

"For God's sakes where, Cassandra, are you all right?"

"Over here, Barry," I call. I begin to pull myself up. I brace myself. I put a hand on the leather padding, and hoist myself to a standing position. But my balance is shaky.

"Are you in the balloon?"

"I'm here, Barry."

"For God's sake, Cassie, what are you doing in the balloon?"

I start to wave. This is slightly more momentum than I'm really prepared for, however. Then too, there's a wind. In any case, my balance is lost, and in reaching for support, I reach too high or too low. I reach just high enough to touch the wrong thing, which is finally the point. The flame increases with an awful roar. There's a series of sounds, like a furious little storm. The basket tips, strains, rocks back and forth like a cradle, rights itself in its moorings, then one of the moorings snaps, and the basket begins to rise. I scream and clutch a cable. Barry shouts, or screams as well, who can tell? Suddenly I'm fifteen or twenty feet off the ground. The basket's at an angle. Everything's askew. "Christ," Barry calls to me. "Hold on. Just hold on, Cassie. And whatever you do, don't move. Don't touch anything else, are you listening?"

"What should I do?" I ask him.

"There in front of you. Do you see them? They're shaped like champagne bottles. Do you see them, Cassie?"

I tell Barry I see them. "Move the right one forward," Barry calls. "Gently. Just a little."

I do what he tells me. "Now," he says. "Look straight overhead. There's a valve. Do you see a valve?"

"I see several valves, Barry."

"The middle one, Cassie. The one in the middle. Turn it counter-clockwise."

I turn it, but I turn it the wrong way, I suppose, for there's a jolt, another blast, and the basket rises another five or six feet.

"No!" Barry calls to me. "No. Forget it. Don't touch anything else, Cassie. Do you hear me? Not a thing now."

"Don't panic, Barry. Watch. See?" I turn the same valve I've just touched. The basket rocks, just as it did before. I chuckle. "There's no harm done."

"I'm going to get help. Just don't panic, Cassie. We're going to get you down from there."

Something in the way Barry says this makes me think of fire trucks with their endless ladders, of kittens out on a limb. Of searchlights and sirens. Of those trampoline-like hoops that firemen hold beneath suicides perched on ledges. I don't know what he has in mind, of course. Not firemen, no doubt. Not that. But I think of a fire company all the same, of grown men in back-billed, funny hats and oily looking slickers, of someone in a great deal of trouble, a burning bed, a monumental leap, a four-alarm life-change that they hadn't been expecting, and that makes Barry seem silly to me. Dear, perhaps — but silly. All of his fears seem out of proportion. I'm not in need of saving. I feel no need of a rescue brigade. I feel, if anything, rather pleased with myself, and surprised. Who else could have managed this particular predicament?

I'm high off the ground, and my fear of heights is substantial. But I don't feel like I'm high off the ground. A fear of heights is really a fear of falling, and I don't envision an imminent fall. I feel buoyed and tethered, and just far enough out of all earthly reach to be safe from harm. I'm levitational, unthreatened. In other words, Barry, I like things just as they are. I like you looking up at me, unsure of yourself, looking toward the house, then looking back to me, embarrassed for us both. I like looking out over rooftops. It has never seemed important before that all of our rooftops were tiled, but, here, aloft, the tiles in the moonlight seem measured and aligned. There's something to be said for measurement in our lives. It's good for the soul. Don't you think?

"Don't go, Barry. Don't leave me."

"What do you think you're doing, Cassie?"

"I'm not sure I want to come down, Barry. That's all. Does that surprise you? Not just yet. Not now that I've had a chance to think about it."

"What are you talking about, Cassie? Are you drunk? Are you out of your mind?'

"Can't I say when I want to come down? Why must everything be your decision, Barry?"

I reach up and give the little valve a twist. There's a burst of flame that's magnificent, yellows on blue. The bottom of the basket is covered in leather, a leather covering over a solid, hardwood section, and I can feel the burst in my toes, then the sense of elevation. The balloon lifts off, then settles and sways.

"All right, Cassandra, don't do that again. Don't do anything you'll be sorry for later. All right. Now what are we talking about here? What is it you have on your mind? What is it you want?"

Oh-oh. I see. We're trying to have an adult conversation. Okay. Okay. Just give me a minute. Let me shake off some of this dope.

What is it I want? Let me put it this way, Barry. If my life were a fish right now, I'd have to throw it back. No? Okay. Seriously then. Here we go. A baby. I want a baby. You're right: I have no interest in raising a child.

Then, a life to match the wardrobe I keep shopping for. Silks, linens, black silk on white silk, bone on top of bone.

A man. A man other than you, in other words, you who I can face in sickness, doldrums, skin eruptions. Oh, come on, who am I kidding? Don't have hurt feelings, in other words: it's you I'd probably choose in the end. Have you heard enough? Are you bored yet? Why is there nothing on cable TV anymore? I feel like the Baby Boomers used up all the really great stories with the happy endings. How's that fair, what's that all about?! Have you looked at the Guide for tomorrow night? *Making It (1982). Young dancers trying to make it in the big city.*

"Barry, do you know how it makes me feel when you have to ask me what I want?"

"What should I ask you then?"

"Something else."

"What are your dreams? Should I ask you that, Cassie? You used to want to be a writer, tell me what you want now, I'd be interested to hear. Tell me a secret. Tell me something you've never shared with another living soul."

Tell you a secret? I think I'm going to check our entertainment unit, I think Barry may have TiVoed Oprah or Dr. Phil. I think he's been sneaking downstairs late at night and watching them both while I'm asleep. Don't trust them, Barry. Those shows are a lie. I'll give you an example. For every woman who longs for an orgasm there are two who long to move their bowels. Am I getting through to you? Am I taking the romance out of this for you?

"I have no dreams, Barry."

"Do you want to change gyms?"

"Try again."

"What are your ambitions? A writer, that's what you used to — "

"I want to be everything you want me to be."

"What's that?"

"What you want me to be? I haven't the foggiest idea, Barry, and I'll tell you the truth, I really don't care. I was being sarcastic."

"What should I ask you?"

"Barry, from the air, in a balloon, does the earth look the way it looks when you're flying in a plane? Does it look to be set out in regular shapes after years of talk and planning?"

"Yes, I suppose you could say that it does."

"And does a cloud look the way it does from a plane, like a fog?"

"You try to avoid the clouds, Cassandra. What is it you're trying to say?"

"Was that a stupid question, Barry? You make it sound as though the question was stupid. Then you ask a question. Go on. I'm listening."

"Cassie, you're going to be so embarrassed about this. I don't know how you think you're going to face our friends."

I haven't even thought about our guests, the party, though a few of them have come out on the lawn, I see, and have taken seats on the grass. This is what Barry has meant for me to see, I imagine, which helps to explain his last statement, a reminder to me that there are friends to face — that every situation has its public dimension. That there is no personal moment you cannot live to regret.

One of our friends says, "Say, you two aren't having a row out here, are you?"

"It's all right if you are," says a woman nearby.

"We wouldn't want to miss a good, juicy row."

There's little commotion, surprisingly. No one seems to think it's strange that I'm up here and they're down there on the ground. The mood is rather convivial. It's a party within a party, which is sometimes how things go. A few clink their glasses and talk among themselves. It's too dark to pick out faces, too poorly vantaged when you're suspended in the dark. The floodlights are nothing but a diamond-like glare from this high overhead. I have to squint to see through this. Someone goes back inside. To Barry he says, "Call out if it gets ugly, will you do that Barry old boy?"

"What's going on, Barry?" I hear someone ask.

"Cassie won't come down until I ask her a question," says Barry.

"I don't get it."

Barry says, "Cassie wants me to ask her a question."

"What question do you want him to ask you?" I'm asked.

I answer, "It's up to Barry."

"What's that Cassie said? I didn't quite catch it."

"Cassie says that it's up to Barry."

The woman I saw on the stairs says, "Can we help him out? Is that allowed, or what?"

Someone else says, "What sort of questions?"

"Questions about herself, I think," says Barry. "Is that about the size of it, Cassie, is that what you have in mind?"

"Not intimate questions, surely."

A man says, "Tell her that you love her."

Barry says, "Cassie already knows that, don't you, Cassie?"

"Yes," I say, "I know that."

The same woman who spoke before says, "I have a question you can ask, Barry. Why are all little piggies pink?"

"I don't know," says Barry. "Let's check with Cassie. Cassandra, did you hear the question? Elaine wants to know why all little piglets are pink?"

"Say," says someone, "this could be fun." There's a round of laughter at this, at so many possibilities, then someone else says, "What if Cassie gave us the answer, then we tried to come up with a question to match it? Maybe that would get us started."

The same person says, "These questions, Barry. Are they matters of fact, or matters of opinion?"

"Barry," I say, "Does any of this make sense to you?"

"Wait a minute," says someone. "Let Cassie talk. Ask your question again, Cassie."

I say, "We were all suppose to feel safe here."

"What are you talking about?" asks Barry.

"This," I answer. "It wasn't supposed to be like this. It was supposed to be different."

"The party? The evening? What's on your mind, Cassandra?"

"All of it. Everything."

Someone says to Barry, "She wants you to know if being safe makes sense to her, I think."

Someone else says, "What?"

"No. I think Cassie's asking why she doesn't feel safe."

"No, that's not what she means" — this is Elaine again, I think.

"I think she's trying to come to some sort of understanding with you, Barry."

"Watch out for those understandings," someone warns Barry.

This brings on a little more laughter, and other little

quips, then a quiet settles over the lawn, or at least it sounds quiet from here. All I can hear is the steady flammable sound of the burner overhead, and the sounds of the birds in the distance. There's a wet smell of grass in the air which seems to me to be rising, a smell of morning, of dawn. Though I have no idea what time it is, it is not late enough in the night to be verging on morning, I know. I listen for the sounds of the loons (loons?) near the reservoir. Is it the loon or the cuckoo that makes its home in another bird's nest? Now there's a question, Barry. At any rate, I don't hear them, these loons, these cuckoos, these feathered friends that malinger along the waterline, waiting to mate. Is there a reason for that, or am I making too much of my own incapacities?

"Cassie," says Barry. "I'll tell you what. I have a party here to host. I've had enough of this now. I'm going inside. When you're ready to come down, you tell us. Just call out, and we'll help you bring it down."

"Are you sure?" someone asks him.

"Barry, there's no telling what she might do."

Barry takes a step closer, separating himself from everyone else. He looks up at me and asks, "Really, Cassie? Are they right? Are you planning on just sailing away? Where do you think you're going to go, Cassandra?"

"I haven't given that much thought, actually," I tell him.

"You don't know how to pilot," Barry says, lowering his voice. "You don't know anything about lift, or the winds. You'll kill yourself, Cassandra. This is all so damned — foolish. Come down from there right now."

I don't like Barry's tone of voice, so when I speak, I call out, look beyond him. "Hey — Somebody — Which way is the wind blowing?" I ask.

"East," someone says. "No, southwesterly."

"What's in that direction?" I ask. "The Pacific Ocean? Is that the way West?"

"The desert, Cassandra. Mexico, west is *that* way," says Barry. There's disgust in his voice at the thought of a desert, or maybe it's my geography.

"How can you tell Mexico from the air?" I ask. "What would it smell like? Does it smell as though it's safe?"

Someone other than Barry says, "What, Mexico? Like cactus, I'd say. Unbearable heat. Sand. Unbearable poverty. Whatchamacallit — sage."

"Iguana dung," someone says, and, don't ask my why, but there's laughter.

"What would it sound like?"

"Cassie wants to know what Mexico sounds like, Barry."

Barry says, "It's a foreign country, Cassandra. It doesn't *sound* like anything."

I look up at my bedroom window, where Sally has perched. Powell is at her shoulder. He has his arm around Sally's shoulder, and the two of them are looking at me, then Sally's holds up her glass, *To The Minstrels*, then I look back at Barry. He's started to gather the guests together. He's trying to get their attention. "My friends," he says, "my friends. I want to apologize for this. Cassie's just had a little bit too much to drink, that's all."

"Like all the rest of us," a male voice calls out. There's laughter at this.

"Right," says Barry, "like all the rest of us. But sooner or later she's going to sober up, and then she's going to be very embarrassed. Now, I think what we should do is to go back into the house, and give Cassie a chance to come to her senses."

A man I saw arrive in a Saab says, "Do you think so? She won't do anything foolish, will she?"

"Cassie? No," says Barry. "Cassie has a flare for the dramatic, that's all. It's one of the things we all love about her."

There's a smattering of polite applause.

"But in the end," Barry goes on, "Cassie's a sensible girl. She just lets herself get out of hand, sometimes. And this, I suppose it's very obvious by now — this is one of those times. So let's all go back inside and carry on. There's still plenty of food, plenty of liquor. And if we start to run low, we'll send out for more, I give you my word."

This doesn't work at first. People are still milling about and kidding Barry good-naturedly about the Hearrons' memorable soirees. Soon, though, Barry begins to corral people, and he gets them back inside. I hear that someone has gone to the piano and they've begun to play show tunes. This means we're trying to impress people tonight, that the crowd is older than usual. I look up to my bedroom. Powell and Sally are gone.

Finally it's just Barry and me. He has his hand on the door. He shakes his head. He means by this that I am beyond understanding, that I've ruined the evening, that I've humiliated us both. "I'll leave this open, Cassandra, so that we can hear you when you call. Whenever you're ready to join us, we'd be pleased to have your company."

I don't do anything for a quite a long while. I just stand there in the wicker gondola, listening to the flame. He means to make me feel unclaimed, undecided, and that's just how I feel, Barry's right — it has worked. Then something amuses me. A man I don't recognize, one of the guests, comes out on the patio, completely oblivious to what has just happened. He takes a napkin from his pocket. It's filled with a canape he's stolen. He looks down at his canape in the strangest way, turning it over, then sniffing it. Is it poison? Has it been dropped in the dirt? Has he never seen one before and he thinks it's coin-operated? Why does he have to steal it to enjoy the act of eating it? Does he think he has no right to things that are his for the taking? I laugh. I've laughed loud enough for him to hear me, apparently, for he gives me a little wave, knowing he's been caught. Then he shrugs his shoulders and goes back to the party.

That's what I see as the balloon begins to rise, just the shrug of his shoulders, then the back of his head. The wind picks up. The balloon rocks a bit to the left and the right. I hang on for dear life as it rises in the air, but I loosen my grip as it settles itself, for a balloon's like anything else, it seeks its proper ballast. It rises, settles, floats then sways — balloon like.

Barry has come back onto the patio. He's leaning against a post that supports one end of an overhang. He's seen this too. He has his feet crossed, and he's holding a drink, a smile spreading over his lips. He walks toward where I am. "Having fun, Cassandra?" Barry asks me.

I shake my head No.

"Is there something you'd like to say to me?"

"Why aren't we safe, Barry? We were all suppose to feel safe here. That was the promise. Has everyone forgotten that?"

"We are safe, Cassie. Look around you. We're in the safest part of city. We have our own Security Patrol, we have our own alarm system. We have floodlights, sirens, our own security cameras. We live in a gated community, Cassandra. I don't know where you think we could live that would be any safer than where we are at the moment."

"I don't think so, Barry. I really don't. I don't think just because some place is gated you can call it a community."

"I do. I belong here. And so do you. Look. Cassie. You've just had a little too much to drink, and now you've started to panic. That's all that's really happened here."

I shake my head No again.

"No? Are you planning on staying out here all night, then? It's getting windy, you realize. There's no telling what might happen."

I say, "Maybe later, Barry.""

I watch as Barry returns to the party. Although he's facing the house, he's still speaking to me, or maybe it's to himself he's speaking. But, in any case, I can hear him say, "Okay. Have it your way. Whenever you're ready, we'll gladly take you back."

## The Fattest Woman On Earth's Near Death Experience, In Which The Fine American Actor F. Murray Abraham Is Mistaken For Parcheesi

The Fattest Woman On Earth, Colorado Holton, was a devout Pentecostal who believed in eternal salvation which began by being whisked toward the heavens in a breathless, thermonuclear glow, but there was none of that when she passed away, none of that cockamamie-instantaneous-out-of-body transcendence-coming-in-a-radiant-shower-of-light. There was no levitation, no rising toward the ceiling when her heart stopped beating in the emergency room. No *sublime*. To the contrary. She was just lying there dead, six days shy of her thirty-first birthday, this in Wheeling, West Virginia, and turning cold as a carp. Was this what death was actually like, she wondered, the ultimate disappointment? She'd been fully prepared to surrender her title as The Fattest Woman On Earth once there were no longer a heartbeat nor pulse, the moment Colorado Holton herself was no longer. She'd been prepared to pass it along to Marla Karnes Higgenbotham of Cape Girardeau, Missouri, at 632 pounds not much more than willowy, relatively speaking, or even Sylvia "Laughing" Martinez of Guadalajara, Mexico, a 535-pound welterweight. And now that that moment was here?

Much of Colorado Holton's life had seemed like a cruel joke, and what if this was the cruelest joke of all? What if beyond a certain bulk weight (something arbitrary, say three-hundred thirty one pounds for women, four-hundred and twenty eight for men) fat does more than clog the arteries and overtax the heart? What if her girth had swelled her soul and enlarged her spirit to the point that gravity held them in place? All these years she'd imagined death would free her from her body, would let some other poor woman wear the mantle of humiliation that she could no longer bear. But death didn't seem to be releasing Colorado in the least. She'd dreamt of rising toward the pearly gates of a diaphanous heaven where she would claim her place among the blessed and beloved. She'd seen her soul levitating in crepuscular, weightless splendor, rising among the souls of drag queens (and drag *kings*, if there were such things), as well as those of burlesque dancers, tap dancers, ventriloquists, fire acts, mazurka dancers, cabaret singers and lip synchers, contortionists, fetish performers, balancing acts, magicians, borsch belt comics, talentless improv troops, lap dancing strippers, jugglers, lounge singers, baton twirlers, body piercers, clowns, hula hoop acts, sword swallowers, aged rock stars, dominatrixes and also submissives, the freaks of the world to which the rest of us feel superior.

She'd dreamt of how her soul would kneel at the feet of God's unfathomable goodness —*Lord God Almighty, Praise Jesus, Saved at last!* — only to discover there was no throne of Divinity, no high celestial gathering, nothing here to look at but a water-stained, acoustical tile ceiling in the Ohio Valley General emergency room. Even when the electrical activity ceased first in her cerebral cortex as if someone had unplugged a lamp cord and then a millisecond later shut down subdurally, this the point when (medically speaking) life ends, when life is irrevocably finished and (Pentecostally speaking) the afterlife begins, Colorado Holton felt no better off than ever, no nearer salvation than she'd ever been, for she was still what she'd been for years, at 772 pounds, The Fattest Woman On Earth. In other words, Colorado experienced her brain's final synaptic skips-to-the-loo not as a moment of sharp transcendent light and sweet emancipation but rather as one more earthly joke being played at the expense of the fat chick.

Then Colorado had the first of two out-of-body experiences, neither of which corresponded to anything she had ever imagined death might be like, much less what she had read about coming back to life after visiting the other side. The first of these defied articulation. The crepuscular light I've mentioned seemed to be not heavenly at all but rather coming in the room from a hospital corridor behind her, yet Colorado didn't cast a shadow, and when she rose from the gurney to examine herself it was like watching a ghost in search of somewhere to haunt. This wasn't an *experience* so much as it was a *transitional moment* during which she was neither alive nor dead, either one. Think of this moment as a *minor disconnect* maybe, not exactly physical but not exactly spiritual either, just odd and disconcerting. As she would later describe it, it was as if Colorado Holton had found herself in a noisy, dimly lit room and someone she knew had directed her attention toward two men in the corner playing a board game. It was as if someone she knew and trusted, a family member, for instance, had remarked, "Isn't that F. Murray Abraham," to which Colorado had answered "Excuse me?" to which the answer had come, "Over there," to which Colorado Holton, still not sure of the question, had answered, "No, that's a game of Parcheesi."

The second experience came fast on the heels of the first, and while it was less obscure, it was no less confusing: The overworked intern throwing up his hands, then thinking better of his decision and making one last attempt to save the patient's life, casually retrieving the defibrillation paddles from where the nurse had placed them in mountings on the wall of the emergency room, the intern saying something that sounded to Colorado like "Ratz Sass," this repeated to the nurse at the exact moment he took in his hand once again the apical paddle, "I don't give a rat's ass, it won't hurt to try," he said to the nurse, the same nurse who had been complaining throughout the resuscitation attempt about having to lash three identical gurneys together in order to make a palette wide enough to work on. Suddenly Colorado could see again, she could hear, she could feel. She could feel herself rising, in fact. It was not as she'd imagined, a bodiless passage at once ethereal and light, but rather a massive and corporeal ascent. That was the thing, how slowly she rose. How incrementally. She was aware of her height, her weight, her mass, never before had she felt herself to be such a huge presence in the world, in fact, yet she was free of space, free of time. If she could count off the seconds by watching a digital clock on the wall as she ascended, how could she feel free of time? If Colorado could watch the nurse drop her hideously flowered surgical tam on the dull and scarred linoleum, how could she feel free of space? And at last Colorado understood. It wasn't death that was freeing, but survival. Living was the miracle, not some mystical curtain of light. Breathing *was* transcendence. This was what she thought to herself as she rose toward the ceiling incrementally, like an ocean liner in a lock: Drawing breath was everything holy. She cleared her mind of all but that thought as she came back to life. Then she rose, and she rose, and she rose.

# Love in the Time of Paris Hilton

## I.

Tailor's sister Taylor introduces me to her best friend Paige who says, "Yesterday I saw my brother pumping our aunt in the shower. We stay with her. Not all the time but, you know, off and on."

"How do you do," I reply.

I ask Paige how long she's known Taylor. Paige can't hear the question over the din of the music, or maybe she just doesn't care. Finally Taylor answers for her. "Most of her pathetic life, girl," says Taylor, putting quotation marks around "pathetic" or "life," or, for all I know, maybe *girl*.

I ask Taylor, "Is Paris here yet, I don't see her."

"Part-Taye, Par-Taye," says Paige, returning to the dance floor.

"Bust a *Par-Taye*," repeats Taylor, following after.

We're as far west as you can go in L.A., smack-dab on the coastline. We've pushed Western Expansion to its mother-bleeping limits, we've fled as far as this country can flee, Santa Monica, near Venice Beach, cater-cornered from the Santa Monica Pier, middle distance between Malibu and Venice itself. We're facing onto the Pacific and a concrete path where inline skaters scull effortlessly.

The music's so loud you have to shout to make yourself heard, so I shout at my date, "How did your mother get Paris Hilton to agree to come tonight, Tailor?"

Tailor smiles at me disarmingly — he has a full, open smile of the sort you may see only three or four times in your entire dating life — then puts his hand at the small of my back. All of this feels a little like ballroom dancing, the way he's been guiding me with his hand since we met several minutes ago. There's a small electric shock when he loses me for a minute then makes contact again. A perfectly pleasant sensation.

He has just turned eleven.

Tailor shouts, "The band's named Houghmagandy. You've read Nabokov, I assume."

"You're eleven years old, what are you doing reading Nabokov?"

"The other band's over there. You can't have too many."

Everyone's dancing suggestively, the girls more so than the boys, but come on, who are we kidding, these aren't "girls" at all, these are ripe, luscious babes booking discount fares on the hand basket to Hell, and way in advance. I mean, in a room this size with this many people? Let these girls loose and we're talking I.E.Ds strapped bandoleer style across their perky little boobs as they crash through the gates of an American embassy — Jihad? Heeee-Hawww! I mean, this is no joke.

Jude has rented the ballroom of this magnificent hotel for her daughter's Sweet Sixteen party and I must be nearly twice the age of any girl dancing. At twenty-eight, I feel it — every year. Just to keep from losing Tailor in the crowd I have to fend off a fifteen-year-old cutie in Juicy Couture jeans who's stripping down to a tank top and her take-me-if-you're-man-enough red stiletto heels, a drunk, nocturnal girl with cage fighter eyes who's in such total possession of her body that she looks right through me when by accident I step on her foot and then ask to be excused. This is Panther — about whom, more later.

"Middle schoolers," shouts Tailor. "They tag along. What are you gonna do?"

Panther says to Tailor, "Bite me, little man. Who's this, your *date*? Great outfit."

"Thanks," I respond.

"Are all your clothes shiny?"

"This way, Cassie," says Tailor.

"Is she another of your sister's friends?"

"My sister has no friends. That's the bar. There."

"Are there really two bands, Tailor?"

"What? I was making a joke about excess. There's the buffet, behind all those kids."

"I can't hear a word you're saying. Can we get a visa and just get cross the border?"

"What?"

"Never mind — Here comes your mother."

Tailor's mother Jude takes two flutes of champagne from a passing tray, seemingly out of her reach, two flutes in one graceful feline gesture that balances all, spilling nothing. One she puts in my hand, the other in her son's, and shouts, "We'll be having one of these for you before long."

"But it won't be at someplace like this," he assures me. "It won't be like this at all."

"How are you two getting along?" asks Jude. "Getting

to know one another?"

"We were on our way to the buffet," I say to no one in particular.

Jude asks, "Have you tried the sushi bar? It's the only thing fit to eat."

Tailor brushes this away. "Jude, isn't that someone from the catering staff? He's trying to get your attention."

Tailor tries several more diversionary tactics to uncouple me from his mother, one lamer than the next, until at last he hits pay dirt. "Oh my God! Isn't that Paris Hilton, Jude?"

"Where?"

"Over there. Near the ice sculpture."

"Which ice sculpture, there's more than one."

"The one on the right."

"The abstract?"

"The Ode To Grief. Why don't you go see?"

Before the question is out of his mouth, Jude seems to vanish. It's as if she's been hoisted off the floor a few inches — one of the privileges apparently of being the hostess tonight is a celestial dispensation from gravitational pull — for the crowd gives her room and she floats through the dancers. We cross in her wake, discovering the buffet by pure chance. There are so many kids.

Tailor surveys what's before him. "Where do you suppose they keep the cutlery? You're my mother's Pilates instructor then?"

"Who told you that?"

"How much is she paying you to be here tonight?"

"The same thing I charge for Pilates, a hundred-and-fifty an hour."

"Thanks for not lying. I couldn't get a date. That's Yellow Tail Sushi, the first one you come to."

"The sign says Inside Out California Roll."

"It's a trick," Tailor says conspiratorially. "Are you into eel?"

"I don't think I've ever had it."

"Tonight might not be the best time for your first taste of eel then."

"It's crowded, isn't it."

"Appearances to the contrary not withstanding, Cassie, my sister has faith in the possibilities of spoken language and real meaning."

"Excuse me?"

Putting the knife and fork in his pocket after allowing me to move ahead of him in line, Tailor hangs a pair of quotation marks in the air.

He's mocking his sister, who has an annoying habit of setting off things she says in imaginary quotation marks, sometimes so often in the same exchange that you can't be sure what is being quoted, not to mention that she is overly fond of the words "like" or "something like that," the first which comes at random and the last which seems to suggest that language is without precision, the presumed relationship of signified and signifier having ended some time ago in a bloody divorce, a divorce so long overdue that finding meaning in a conversation is a fool's errand to begin with, the quotation marks in this case setting off "fool's" or "errand," there's no telling which.

"Your sister calls your mother *Jude*," I say. "So do you."

"Well, that *is* her name — As far as we know. Would you like a plate?"

"No, I meant — Is she your stepmother or something?"

"I don't think so. Why don't you just put the champagne down if you're not going to drink it."

"So how did she get her to come?"

"Paris Hilton? Three years ago it was Matt Damon. Last year? Julie Taymor. Jude's a casting agent, she throws lots of parties. She invites whoever is current."

His sister elbows her way to where we're waiting in line. Tailor greets his sister with such effusive insincerity that it can only be pulled off by the *fin de siècle* social scions of Henry James or Edith Wharton, but for someone who doesn't yet shave, he doesn't do badly, I have to admit. "Why Taylor, you're back, how pleasant to see you again, sister dear. Would you like a plate, or will you behave as if we're at home and just treat all this as a trough?"

"Can I cut in front, like do you mind, Cassie?"

"It's *your* Sweet Sixteen," I say, stepping back. "Doesn't it ever get confusing?"

"I'm confused all of the time," says Tailor, "about everything, almost everything confuses me. That happens once you're alive."

"I meant your names. There must be so many mix-ups."

His sister looks at me blankly. "In what sense?"

"You're both named *Taylor*, right?"

"She spelled mine with a Y," she answers.

"She spelled mine like someone who hems. You know, like a tailor."

"I can see how that would clear things up."

"She thinks before she acts," he says.

"It's a kind of Faulkner thing," says his sister. "Like *Sound and the Fury?*"

"Jude's very into Faulkner," says Tailor. "Or maybe it's someone else."

"Well great, okay. So there you are — So there'll be no Paris Hilton tonight, or there will, which is it?"

Taylor explains to me, helping herself to a plate, "Think of Paris Hilton as this year's basic black."

Her brother, thinking aloud, says, "Julie Taymor would have been all right to meet."

"In any case, don't get your heart set on meeting Paris Hilton," Taylor cautions me. "They never show up."

"Never," says Tailor.

"Not once," adds his sister, then she looks at the buffet and says, "Don't fill up on this crap. There's sashimi at the very end."

"Paris Hilton isn't coming? *Bummer*," says Tailor. "And there's Caesar salad on the other side."

"Are you pretending not to care?" asks Taylor.

"*Please.*" Her brother turns to me, aware I suppose that sushi's not my idea of food. "Nothing looks good?"

I point toward something that should be on a wall of the Getty Museum. "What's Rainbow Roll?"

"No Paris Hilton. My life's ruined — My sister, bearer of all bad news."

"Oh God, there's Mona," she replies.

A woman in her forties wearing a too-tight Chelsea Handler T-shirt is dancing with a boy named Phil. She's been putting her best moves on young Phil, who looks like he might be much more comfortable in black chiffon than any of the girls here. Mona must be having the same thought, for she signals to some girls she sees to join her, a girl named Padgett, then Paige, and some other girls, and they begin dancing as a group.

"Who's Mona again?" I ask.

Taylor says, "Paige's aunt. You'll stay away from her if you know what's good for you."

Tailor makes fun of his sister. "You may have age on your side but Mona has conviction on hers." Then he seems genuinely concerned for my safety. "But Taylor's right, Cassie, I'd keep my distance tonight."

Tailor goes into a long story, only part of it intelligible. The jist is that Mona has been getting it on with her nephew Rap like it's going out of style, someone Tailor introduced me to earlier, a sweet kid in a Lacoste blazer with a goofy expression and a slightly demented grin. "Don't say you haven't been warned," he adds.

"I've definitely been warned."

He points toward a couple at the cusp of the dance floor. "He used to go out with Panther. That's Rap, remember? Paige's brother. Mona's nephew." Rap and a girl are doing something with their bodies that has nothing to do with the music's bass line much less a drummer. Part stumble, part rage, it is less a choreographed dance than invisible jolts of electricity that send you into contortions. Recover from one, and they jolt you with the next.

"Rap. Right. I remember now."

Jude has been negotiating the dance floor with enviable ease, like she's riding one of those little hover boards from "Back To The Future," all of this on behalf of Paris Hilton's arrival, explaining to some of the entourage the standards of behavior. *Standards of behavior*, that is, for when — deep breath! — Paris finally gets here. All of this with a kind of breathless excitement. Beat, beat. Exhale.

"When Paris gets here," says their mother, as if catching her breath after just setting foot on the surface of the moon, "don't let on like you notice, okay? Act like you're unimpressed."

"I am unimpressed," says Taylor.

"I'm sorry, what did you just say young lady? Did you just say something silly?" Jude flashes a smile while she awaits a good answer.

I whisper to Tailor, "Is that a hint of dissent I sense?"

"The social fabric is only as good as its strongest thread," he informs me.

The last part of this Jude overhears, I think, just as Tailor is turning away, so Jude flashes in my direction that fuck-with-me-at-your-own-peril smile of hers. "Let's get better acquainted, Cassie I feel like I hardly know you. You're from Toledo, right?"

"St. Louis, originally. I just moved here from Arizona. I've been here six months."

"What else do you do besides work in a Pilates studio?"

"She's written a screenplay," says Tailor.

"How do you know that?" I ask.

"It's a safe bet. Think about where you're living."

"I don't have an agent yet."

"Where's it set?" asks his mother.

"In Europe. It's a really great story with a happy ending."

"In Europe, not L.A.?" Taylor asks.

"In France and Spain," I explain. "In the 19th century."

"Some kind of Johnny Depp vehicle, right?" Jude says, looking at me with pity.

Tailor says, "Sooner or later, you'll write about L.A."

I don't bother to say that he couldn't be farther from

the mark. I don't say I can only take L.A. in small doses, and my interest in this city and those who call it home can be best described as morbid curiosity. And I don't say *I couldn't* write about it, it's less a matter of choice than of temperament. I couldn't even make fun of it, or do what Nathaniel West did. I just don't see the grand dame of bright dreams and dim prospects that haunted Scott Fitzgerald. For me, there is no romance of the Day-Of-The-Whatever, Hopelessness-Of-It-All variety. I wouldn't know where to begin.

Finally, I don't say I'm offended on principle by the comfort L.A. finds in its own absurdity; I think this city is a waste. I wouldn't be here if I weren't using the money I got in my divorce settlement to stake a writing career. I've run as far away from common sense and my plans for the future as my settlement would take me, and now here I am in L.A., never quite sure if L.A. is a love-starved girl driven to be thin, or just a fluty old queen in a tacky get-up, but either way I can't see the appeal.

Come on. Paris Hilton? Tailor and Taylor? Think about it. You can't make that up, why try?

What I say instead is, "I doubt it, I really do."

Jude says, "Trust me. Everyone writes about L.A. eventually."

"And why's that?"

Tailor says, "L.A. is to America what America is to the rest of the world."

"So easy to feel superior to," says Taylor.

"See there?" says her mother, flashing me her smile. "It's common knowledge."

For a split second it's me more than Taylor who is being

dissed for the old silly-quotient, and I imagine all the times Jude must have flashed that smile since motherhood, a devalued currency by this point, a kind of mouth within a mouth, lips too thin to hide the strain anymore, a smile that says "Kids, what are you gonna do, God love'em," but the one inside screams out "Surrender, Dorothy. Goddam You, Surrender!"

"I asked you what you said, Taylor," she says, turning to her daughter.

"Skip it," says Taylor. Luckily she's let out of the dog-house still quicker than she was put there, for Jude is on to other matters — namely me.

"Tell me, Cassie, do you think you're better than the rest of us too? Then just go on with what you're doing. Pretend not to care."

"That won't be easy," says Tailor.

"I'd love to meet Paris Hilton," I say, "I think it's exciting."

Jude says to me, "You have no idea what a nightmare it is to keep the paparazzi at bay, not to mention those syphilitic dwarves from *Entertainment Tonight* or *L.A. Weekly.* Oh shoot, there's —" Jude snaps her fingers repeatedly, trying to summon up the name and put it with a face, then seems to have been spirited away as if by the call of that process.

Tailor says, "You'd love to meet her, Cassie — What a crock!"

I ask, "Who's the woman your mother is talking to now? I've seen her on TV."

Tailor says to his sister, "Doesn't Jude look buoyant!"

"And after all she's been through."

"What's she been through?" I want to know.

Taylor says, "She's an Oscar front-runner."

"Your mother?"

"No, the woman in the wig. Jude's best friend Alex. The woman she's talking to. She's a costume designer. 'Brokeback Mountain,' 'Kissing Jessica Stein.'"

"Alexandra, Alex to her friends — Paige's mother?" says Taylor, clarifying things for herself, if not for me. "*Alexandra*."

"What's with the wig, Taylor?" he asks.

"It's an early stage of chemo," she answers.

"It's an early stage of depression, more likely," says her brother.

Appearing out of thin air, and then disappearing just as quickly, Jude says with absolute authority, "Depression doesn't advance in predictable, orderly stages."

"But then neither do my mother's parties," says Tailor.

"How does she do that?" I ask.

"Just suddenly materialize?"

Tailor says, "We've never really known."

"It's creepy, isn't it," says his sister.

"We're guessing astro-projection."

"How does your mother know Paris Hilton?" I ask.

"Not that she's really coming," says Taylor.

"Not that we'd care if she did," says her brother.

Jude overhears some or all of this as she passes by from yet another direction — no telling how much. She slows her stride and turns on her heels, coming our way, I'm afraid. I take a deep breath, then let it out when we're saved at the last minute by someone who distracts Jude's attention, a heavily moisturized, handsomely booted woman who might well be her twin from this distance. This is Mona, of Pumping Rap Like It's Going Out Of Style fame. This is Mona, Paige's aunt, who says one thing so loud I can hear it over the band, even from here, "Just don't hold your breath." But Jude's not one to be easily distracted. Once she breaks free she gets in her daughter's face and says, "Of course Paris is coming. Don't be silly. Once you have her word, you're golden."

Tailor looks at his watch. "When's she supposed to get here?"

His mother responds, "Anytime now."

"Jude."

"One or one-thirty, at the latest."

I try to get as much of that effusive insincerity into my voice as I can, but clearly I'm an amateur, out of my depth. Jude assumes I'm perfectly serious. "Paris Hilton?"

"Paris *Hilton*," she reassures me.

## II.

"Where should we sit, Cassie?"

"Anywhere but the head table, Tailor, I couldn't take it."

"Over there," says Tailor. "Near the Ode To Grief."

Sweeping past us in the most recent of her low-level sorties, Jude puts her cheek next to mine and says (girl-friend to girlfriend, as if this is the moment we've bonded), "Grief is only for the young, isn't it, Cassie, the rest of us don't have the time."

Tailor says, "It looks like it's filling up fast. I'll save you a place." Tailor takes my plate and goes on ahead.

"Lead the way. I'm right behind you."

I find myself caught in a regiment of frenzied, sex-starved dancers. Rap and his Lacoste insignia appear from the mist like Young Lochinvar, except where Lochinvar might have put me on the back of his steed and ridden brusquely through the loam and the heather, Rap has other ideas. He just wants to dance with someone with breasts. Once this gets started, I can't get away. I'm stuck, for Rap understands *partner* to mean what it means to all boys his age. He gets as close to me as I'll let him and starts pounding his hips. He might be humping a chair.

Just when I think I'll never be released I'm saved by a man with sallow skin and Herman Tarnower eyes who can muster the courtly elegance that only homely men can manage. He asks if he can cut in then moves us off the dance floor a little at a time. He puts his arm around me as if we're about to foxtrot and introduces himself as Taylor's grandfather. I gather from what he's saying that he's a physician with a practice in Westwood, something to do with women. I thank him for protecting me from the barbarous warrior caste, but secretly I resent the fact that he's had to think for both of us.

Later I'll get the skinny. He made a fortune in straightening little girls' spines. He's well known in Scoliosis circles, he's Dr. Spine, he's The Boss, he's to Scoliosis what Bruce Springsteen is to rock and roll, having invented the corrective pedicle screws that are central to that surgery.

Where he really struck gold though was in selling the idea that a woman's carriage is her beauty. I take it his services are to the Oscars what low cut gowns and two-sided tape are to the Emmys. You wouldn't want to be there without them. By fusing together the first twelve vertebrae of a woman's back, T-1 through T-12, he can get you two additional inches of height. And he's not just straightening you out, either. There's a better shift of balance through the hips. He's straightened into a perfect alignment some of most bodacious female vertebrae in this city. Michelle Pfeiffer, Rene Russo. Without him, Naomi Campbell and Jennifer Lopez would both be working at Hooters. He has them all down to less than five percent of curvature, without any rotation at all. How he's hidden the scar is for him to know and for you to find out. Wars have been started over less.

By the time I can join the others, Tailor is sitting at a big table where all the plates are filled and carefully positioned but most of the chairs are empty. The guests who go with them are out on the dance floor or just milling about. There's just Taylor, her brother, and me, and Jude and Alex so far on the other side of the table that they are all but out of earshot.

"Wanna dance?" Tailor asks me, helping me with my chair.

"I'd still be out there if it wasn't for your grandfather."

"He's Taylor's grandfather, not mine. We're two husbands removed. He's here as Mona's date."

"This is the head table."

"Our lucky day. It was this or eat off the floor. Start with the tuna. The fruit is only a garnish, by the way."

"Which one's tuna?"

"I guess you didn't get any. See what Taylor's eating now? Want to try it?"

"Sure."

Tailor passes a bread plate in his sister's direction and says, "Taylor, can Cassie try a taste, just give her a bite so she can see if she likes it."

Taylor allows this half-a-second's thought, then ignores it.

"Whenever it's convenient," says her brother.

"Let her get her own. I'm not her slave," his sister answers.

"Is it convenient yet?" asks Tailor.

"I'm really not comfortable with sharing food," his sister answers. "Besides, I have blood sugar issues."

"I'll go back to the buffet," Tailor says to me.

"Sit still."

"Don't mind Grendel. When she gets like this we just throw a couple of small horned animals into her den, then run for our lives. Seriously, I'll get you some if you'd like to try it."

"Maybe later. First I'll sample what I have."

Panther and Padgett return from the dance floor. As they squeeze themselves behind our chairs in order to get to their own, Panther ruffles Tailor's hair with her fingers and Padgett says, "Having fun, little man? With your *date?*"

Taylor says, "Is that top Chanel?"

Padgett says, "Don't you love how it's ripped."

"I got it online," Panther answers.

Taylor looks askance: "No one wears the same designer their mother wears."

Padgett says, "Panther, does your mother still wear Chanel?"

"Only all the time," says Taylor.

"Ooooooo, gross," says Padgett.

Panther and Padgett fall into a version of Valley Girl speak without a moment's thought. They have perfected the nasal thing, the body language that has disdain for anything not them, *that* attitude, but everything they say comes out of their mouths with a subtle patina of irony. Everything here is META, it's Valley Girl to the second power, like Taylor's punctuation that appears first of all in the air. The point is that she's not the sort of girl who would think to punctuate anything, and Taylor's superior to those who do what she's doing. These are just characters they're playing, clothes they slip in and out of, masks they slip on and off, this in a world where imitation is the sincerest form of mockery.

The next to arrive is Mona and her date, Dr. Spine. Then Jude comes over to see if Taylor is having a good time. Then Alex, left to her own devices, decides it's more interesting sitting next to me than to be abandoned by Jude and left all by herself.

Alex and I bond right away. She introduces herself, moving her plate next to mine. I say I'm not sure I should be here at the head table. It should be for the immediate family, or at least their closest friends. I say I'm going to see if there's an opening somewhere else and she says, "Come on, don't be silly, there's room. Really, Cassie. Think about who's *in* this family. Besides, we're one rat short at the cheese wheel of life."

It's not clear to me from how Alex tells the story how she and Jude met. It seems to be that Alex met Jude when Jude didn't invite her to Alex's wedding — or maybe the other way around. It doesn't make sense, the story. But there are any number of things at this party like that. Like Jude's conviction that Paris Hilton is going to come waltzing through the door at any minute. I ask if Jude's serious, does she really expect her? Alex sets me straight. Her point is, There is no more chance of Paris Hilton showing up tonight than there is of the Clippers winning the Regional Finals or of Godot pulling up in a Hummer, but no one would care if they did. It's just an *excuse* — For what, she doesn't explain. She asks me where I'm from.

"St. Louis, originally. Well a suburb. How'bout you?"

"That's in Missouri, right?"

I acknowledge that it is, or at least it was the last time I checked.

"Missouri. Yeah. I've heard of it."

It's one of those moments when two women make eye contact and know they are friends for life. "Just for the record?" I confide. "I'm here because my asshole of a landlord won't replace the gas-leaking Kenmore range in my shoebox of an apartment. It's the pits, it really is, but it's all I can afford. If I don't get out of there soon, you'll be watching the story on the local evening news: *An As-Yet Unidentified Tennant Goes Out With A Bang. More At Eleven.*"

"*But First, Guess Which Grammy-Winning Diva Has Just Had A Baby.*"

"Exactly. It may only be a few hundred bucks, but that's a lot of money to me right now."

"What are you, an actress?"

"Pilates instructor."

She removes her wig. She's bald. She fans herself with the wig and says, "Is it hot in here, or is it just me?"

"Are you, you know — ?"

"Sick, as in lymphoma? No, nothing so dramatic. I shaved it off. Well, first I used the pinking shears. I'm getting a divorce."

"I'm sorry, I've been through one of those. Is yours tough?"

"It's not the worst thing, not even at my age. Except we're in a custody thing over Paige."

"Look, I barely know you, I shouldn't have brought it up."

"Everyone talks about what divorce can do to a woman's personality. If that's true, what about the opposite, what can your personality do to help you get through the rough spots, right? The real danger's self-revelation. It's easy to despise the butt-head who's claiming the Cuisinart is actually *his*, but what if you learn you're a compulsive, impossible bitch."

I assure her there's no possibility of that. I've just met her, and already I feel like we're sisters. With some people it's just instinctive, I reassure her. I confide that Jude however can be intimidating.

Alex says, "Jude's the sort of woman you don't take to immediately. She takes a while to get to know. But then you think she's fabulous — or you take out a restraining order. She's been great to me through the breakup. I'm not sure I could face this divorce without her, if you want to know the truth. I mean, the whole custody thing. It's charged with emotion."

"What about Rap, is he suing for custody of Rap?"

"No. Rap lives with my sister Mona. So does Paige, of course. My Ex is suing me so I'll have to raise Paige myself."

"Your daughter doesn't live with you?"

"During the school year? How could she? I live in Arizona. Have you ever been to Scottsdale? It's the most wonderful place in the world. You should visit me some time. October through May is ideal, you'll think you've gone to heaven."

"So long as they have a stable home."

"Thank God for Mona."

"Right."

"Raising your own children," she says. "It's just another way of putting women in their place."

# III.

Rap comes over to the table. He asks me to dance, then says hello to Panther. Panther turns to Taylor and says, "Did you hear something? I thought I heard someone say my name. Is it me? Did you hear that too?"

"Come on, Panther," Rap protests.

"I think I need to use the ladies room," Panther says.

Rap says to me, "What do you say, want to dance with me again?"

"Rap," says Alex.

"*What?* I just asked her to dance."

"Maybe you ought to leave Cassie alone right now, Rap," says Tailor.

"No one's talking to you," says Rap, "you dickless wonder. Is she your date?"

"Rap," says Alex. "That's enough now."

Rap shoves Tailor forward, as if he means to push Tailor's face into his plate, and says, "See what kind of twerp you have for a date tonight?"

"Was that suppose to be for my benefit?" I ask Rap.

"I wouldn't say *benefit*," answers Tailor, straightening himself and trying to regain what dignity he can.

"Loser," says Panther, rising from the table.

Rap says, "Come on, Panther, what's with you? I want to talk."

"As if," Paige says, rising as well. Taylor and Padgett follow suit.

Panther says to me, "We're going to the ladies room, Cassie, want to come?"

"Stop being such a pain, Panther," says Rap. He steps in front of her, blocking her way. Panther stares him down.

"Excuse me," she says. Then to me she says, "Are you coming or not?"

I get lucky. I'm the first through the door — "*Whatever before beauty*," Panther tells me — and get in line behind a woman who's actually near to my age. She's the Personal Assistant to someone's mother and has been volunteered as a chaperone this evening. She tells me her name but says it so quickly it sounds like "Wendell Willkie" then launches into a monologue. Her monologue is from that subgenre of Chick Lit I've come to call "Revenge Tragedy." She's been involved with an older man and now they're going through a pretty rough breakup. I don't get all the facts but I gather it was his fault more than hers. She is living by herself at the moment. She went from living under her father's roof to living under his and she is discovering who she is, a freedom as valuable to her as Buccellati gold work.

The best thing about Revenge Tragedy is that it's mercifully short. It is usually under three minutes long from start to finish, which is good, because she divides the rest of her allotted time between explaining to me what she's doing to discover her inner strength, and sobbing. Soon she is crying so hard she has to leave the room entirely.

Behind me, Taylor is going over the fight she was having with Jude at the table. No one is listening, much less responding. "I'm so spoiled. And while I'm confessing? That was me with the guy on the leash in the prison photo, and she can stop hating Yoko Ono because I was the one who broke up the Beatles — I'm tired of being her whipping post."

"Whipping *boy*," I suggest.

"That too. Jude has this way of speaking about us as if

we're strangers who've been caught in a car wreck — have you ever noticed that?"

I say, "You seem more upset than Jude."

"Can't she just die and leave us the money?"

Behind Taylor, Padgett and Paige are into their Valley Girl thing, and Panther is primping in a full-length mirror.

"Gross me out," says Paige.

Panther adjusts her tank top so its Chanel insignia is off to one side and the front is still more revealing.

"Wait till Rap gets a load of those," says Taylor.

"As if," says Panther.

"Who do you think you're talking to, girl?" Paige protests.

Taylor says, "It's not really his fault."

Panther says, "Give me one reason to forgive him."

Taylor says, "He can lick the back of his own neck with his tongue."

"Okay," says Paige.

"Give me *two*," says Panther.

"How long do we have to stay in here?" asks Padgett.

Taylor says, "Until Rap's gone back to his table."

Padgett catches my eyes in the mirror. She says, "Cassie looks like she could use a hot shower."

Taylor says, "She's had that expression on her puss all evening."

"And what expression would that be, I wonder?" I reply.

Paige says, "We've all seen it."

"If you think you're above all this, why don't you leave?" Taylor demands.

"Because unlike you, I need the money."

"But that's not all of it, is it? You're trying to get in good with Jude so she'll help you get an agent. Where do you live, in the Valley?" asks Paige.

"In Silverlake. Half a block east from the Earl Scheib lot, if you know where that is."

"No. Not really."

"Of course not. Silverlake is probably three or four rungs beneath the circles you frequent."

"At-It-TOOOD," says Taylor.

Panther says, "Pardon us for living."

Paige adds, "While you claw your way out of poverty."

Taylor says, "She liked Rap well enough."

Panther says, "You probably Sharon Stoned him. I wouldn't put it past you."

Taylor has to interpret. She explains that Sharon Stone is a game the girls play. You hike up your skirt while sitting in a chair and the first one to attract a boy wins, though there are countless variations, such as several girls Sharon Stoning at the same time at a crowded dance and the winner is the one who can get a boy to walk the greatest distance to hit on her. The rules are flexible, in other words. Like Wiffleball, they can always be adjusted to the number of players and where you happen to be, and, also like Wiffleball, girls outgrow Sharon Stoning at nine or ten.

Panther says, "I'm going to be sick."

Panther gives me a withering look, like she's turned me to salt with one glance, and I assume she's just being bitchy until she covers her mouth with her hand, getting ready to spew. She breaks out of line and forces her way into the next empty stall. She pushes past an attendant, an Ecua-dorian woman in a maid's uniform who has been sitting on a little stool, talking into her cell phone using Bluetooth, a china plate in her lap filled with dollar bills and change.

"Eating disorder?" I ask.

"Please," says Padgett, "that was your generation, not ours."

Paige says, "Maybe someone should help her. Panther needs help."

"Any takers?" says Taylor, looking directly at me.

"Why me?! You're her best friends."

"Because you're being paid to be here and I'm not — Let's start with that. And just for the record? I'm not her best friend. That honor goes to Rap, he's the one who's poking her."

"And also they're in love," says Paige. Padgett nods her agreement.

Panther reappears before anyone has to go in to help her, looking none the worse for wear. She stabs me in the chest with her finger and says, "You just stay away from Rap. Got it? And one more thing: Something's going down tonight."

Adds Paige, "And if you know what's good for you?"

Stepping up with Paige and Panther, Taylor finishes the thought: "You won't want any part of it."

"Understood?" asks Padgett. She does what women do to make each other uncomfortable: she gets one step closer to me than she has any right to. I feel like I'm the fresh meat in one of those Women-Behind-Bars soft-core pornies, the one with the bull dyke guard and the mandatory shower scene, because Padgett gets in my face, then Taylor and Panther crowd me until I'm backed into a corner.

"Make up your mind which side you're on," Paige warns me.

Padgett says, "Why don't you just sit for a while."

"When it starts going down," adds Panther.

"Why, what's going to happen?"

Panther puts her nose inches from mine, knotting my top in her manicured fist. "You'll stay out of it if you know what's good for you."

"And chill," says Taylor.

"Did you just say chill?" asks Paige.

"No one says *chill*," says Padgett.

"Chill. Jesus Christ," says Panther.

## IV.

Anyway, that was about an hour ago. Tailor and I have spent our time dancing or sitting by ourselves at the table, where we've done our best to talk above the noise. We're dancing at the moment and I'm feeling my age. It's past midnight, going on one o'clock. I'm hoping for a slow number.

Everyone on the dance floor seems to be expending a great deal of effort, but to no certain end. Legs tuck back and backs bend side to side. Arms flail with a kind of blithe self-consciousness, but no one is in time to the tump-thudding-thump of the band. Heads and thighs and shoulders go on about their business nonetheless, as if thwarting a master command — the only exception is Padgett.

She's back at the table. Padgett is eating a carrot stick. She's talking — well, actually she's *listening* — to Dr. Spine. He's pouring out his heart, trying to woo her to his bed, and as near as I can tell there is not one whit of human response in her eyes. Not compassion, not discomfort. There's no one home. Zip. Nothing. Disdain is as near as she can come to an emotional threshold. Occasionally she rolls her eyes toward the ceiling in my direction, or forms an L with her right hand, extending her thumb and first finger; this is the Valley Girl sign, worldwide, that your date is a loser, but in this case signals — I think — that geezers like him are her core demographic. Maybe it's not an L at all but a broken-A, for Anna Nicole Smith. Just marry'em and bury'em and get yourself a lawyer.

Padgett takes him by the hand and leads him out to the dance floor. He's willing but creaky. She is leading him to the area where Mona is dancing with Rap. Paige tucks in behind them. Others follow Paige. And you can tell that something is up. Maybe it's how they relate to the music. They seem distanced from the melody but fully in touch with the anger of its lyrics.

The girls form a conga line, hands over their heads though they seem to be watching their feet. Their fingers pantomime a gentle summer rain while from the waist down they could be molesting a PT Cruiser. When they come upon Mona and Rap, the conga line flexes into an arc until it surrounds them.

"Fasten your seat belt, Cassie, and return your seat backs to the upright position," Tailor warns me.

It starts when Panther breaks ranks. After pushing Rap to one side, she goes toe to toe with Mona and says, "You can't spend your whole life splashing in the shallow end of the pool."

Mona doesn't know what to make of this.

"Splashing," says Panther. "Splashing, Splashing, Splashing."

It takes a beat for this to get through. Mona seems bewildered; not scared exactly, but not happy either, she knows this isn't a joke. The circle widens as others join in, boys and girls both. Now Jude is in the middle with Mona, and Alex as well.

Panther says, "You can't spend anymore time in the shallow end. Okay? Understood?!"

"Shallow end," goes the chant, "shallow end."

Panther points her finger at Mona, then at Jude and Alex in turn, and says, "Splashing, splashing." Panther turns to her friends, enlisting their help. She's pumping her arms, she's pumping them up. "Splashing, splashing, splashing."

"Splash-Shing! Splash-Shing! Splash-Shing!!" comes their response.

Beneath this, Panther continues. "Look at yourself, Jude, you look younger than we do. There isn't one mother in this room who hasn't been under the knife, changed the size of her boobs, or botoxed her skin. You all look as if you've been mani/pedi'ed to death, waxed into extinction, rolled and tucked like an overpriced couch. You've all been revised and revamped until there's nothing of you left to work with. If you're ashamed of looking old enough to be our mothers, what does that say about *us*?"

"This has to stop," Jude shouts. "If I let you kids get away with this, why should you ever take me seriously again?"

Panther counters, "What makes you think we take you seriously now?! And something else, Jude: No more skinny jeans. We can wear them but you can't, you look like the butt that ate Bakersfield!"

It's one thing to tell Jude her butt is too big (which it isn't, it's just an age-appropriate butt), but this? Did Panther just say that Jude is not central?

Dr. Spine looks like an old building where the plaster has begun to crack and you can see the lath underneath. Mona is looking scared. Alex can't tell whether to laugh or to cry.

"Vertebrae weren't meant to be fused," Panther screams. "Are you morons?! And you," she says, turning to Alex. "Mothers should raise their own kids. And no more of that Kick-Ass Red nail polish, the world has moved on, you look like you should be walking the streets."

"Enough!" shouts Jude.

Enough? Panther's barely started. Who knows, maybe Panther and these other kids are actually getting through to them.

"Splash-Shing. Splash-Shing. Splash-Shing…"

"Look at how we dress! We're too young to drink, can't you see that?! Are all of you fools? Do any of you care? We're too young for you to be screwing. We're too young to be screwing each other. Why did you have us if you didn't want to raise us? Look at what you've done to your children. Look at what you've done to the air. Look at what you've done to the planet."

"Splash-*Shing*. Splash-*Shing,* Splash-*Shing,* Splash-*Shing,* Splash-*Shing…"*

"There wasn't supposed to be a Nine-Eleven or a George W. Bush. We're doing more harm than good in Afghanistan, we had no business sending troops to Iran, and we never seem to learn, just look at Iraq! Desert Storm was a joke, no one cares how big our dick is, and we never seem to learn, just look at Obama. There's no such thing as a war on terrorism, it's a slogan from Madison Avenue. Going to war is one thing. Terrorism's another. And why do we need protection from the rest of the world to begin with? Al Qaeda has yet to organize a terrorist cell that can kill us any quicker than we are killing ourselves. There's not one person in this room who has any real hope that things will get better than they already are. And that's wrong. Tell me that's not wrong! It's America. You're supposed to have hope that life can get better. And once that hope is lost, something's wrong. You're the adults, not us. How stupid must you be not to know that?!"

"Splash-*Shing*, Splash-*Shing*, Splash-*Shing*."

It's as if these kids are coming alive, for the first time all night, maybe the first time ever, and the way the kids are moving makes you remember how young they actually are. They look like teenage kids. It's as if their years are falling away a layer at a time until they are youngsters once again. Who knows, maybe this is what we've been waiting for. Something or someone has to bring us together. Maybe I'm here at its beginnings…

"SPLASH-shing, SPLASH-shing, SPLASH-ing."

There's something in the air though. What seemed a minute ago to be a chance for renewal has taken on an edge. The chant is getting louder and louder, drowning out Panther and everything else. We're not talking protest. We're not even talking teenage ANGST. This is different. It's hard to put your finger on, but whatever it is, it's mean of spirit and loose of limb.

The chant grows more insistent, more cadenced, and more primal. Then changes entirely. There's no telling what they're saying. I'm not even sure they're words. They're just making noise, maybe BIG FAT WHITE DOGGIE, BIG FAT WHITE DOGGIE. That's not what they're saying, that's just what it feels like, those are its rhythms, and it's growing more insistent. They're clapping their hands, stomping their feet, as if trying to release the room from its moorings with nothing more than their physical presence. Our oracle's out of business. Panther's been diminished to stomping instead.

BIG, FAT, WHITE, DOGGIE, BIG, FAT, WHITE, DOGGIE, BIG FAT…

The circle's closing in. What seemed a few minutes ago to be a means of putting things right now seems like something other. There's hatred here, and it's primitive with a P. Pure, unadulterated hatred. The band begins packing up. Smart move. This party's over.

"Duck," says Tailor, pushing me out of the path of a flying chair. We duck behind an overturned table, pressing ourselves into the sliding glass doors that lead out to the beach. If one of us could find the latch that opens them, we'd be history.

We barricade ourselves as securely as we can behind some overturned tables as Taylor's presents fly overhead like rounds from a mortar. Her brother turns to me and asks, "Did you really grow up in St. Louis, Cassie, or did you just make that up?"

"Born and raised."

"Is that where people have table saws in their basements?"

"We didn't. Our neighbors probably did, I can't really say."

"I'll bet you played touch football in a neighbor's back yard though."

"When I was little. Later the boys wouldn't let me play with them."

"They were making a mistake, Cassie. Duck! Incoming!!"

"What are we going to do, Tailor?"

"Well, under the circumstances, I think the fire department is the best way to go. I'm going to crawl around the edge and look behind the curtains. That's normally where you find the alarms."

"Why not just call the police?"

"You *are* from Missouri, aren't you. Don't go anywhere without me. I'll be back in a minute."

## V.

The firemen arrive in no time. They don't storm through the doors though, they walk single file then mill about for a minute on the edge of the chaos, putting on masks and readjusting their slickers before coming on strong. They look silly just standing there. They look lost and out of place, and something about so much ill-fitting rubber protection makes them seem almost comic, almost marsupial. Once they're ready, however, they're ready; you can feel them revving up.

Just when you think there's nothing left to believe in, no hero we haven't outgrown, you find firemen like these. These are terror-filled times we live in. Anxiety's the norm. Most of us are cowards. Truth be told, most of us are wimps. We're physically lazy, we spend our lives scared. Well not here, not now, not the Los Angeles Fire Department. There's not a lazy bone in their bodies. I'll bet there's not a coward among them. There they are, putting body and limb on the line to save the rest of us, brave and strong and courageous. But let's get down to basics. Do you smell smoke? Where are the flames? There's a problem here. They think they've come to fight a fire, that's what they're prepared for, and they're not going to leave till they find it. Even if that means tearing the place apart. Here come the fire axes. Here comes the hose.

One of the firemen must have severed the wiring of the hotel's emergency system. This must have tripped its alarm for the room goes dark, pitch dark. For twenty seconds or so, we could be in a cave. Then there's a flurry of ONNNK-ONNKing sirens and sweeping searchlights. The searchlights are housed so near the automatic sprinkler system in the ceiling that they have to be turned off quickly by some master switch; if not, the heat sets off the sprinklers. So now the sprinklers are spewing water by the gallons. This confirms to the fire brigade what they've suspected all along, that there's a fire here, probably in the walls, or maybe in the ceiling. They go at it all the harder. They turn their hose on anything that moves.

Meanwhile, Jude gets sucker punched by Dr. Spine, who's trying to get away through the same door she is.

Tailor says, "Oh, good lord, look, someone's called the cops."

"I hope they called more than those two."

"Trust me," says Tailor, "two's more than enough. Someone's going to get killed. Let's just hope it's not us."

These are LAPD. They look a little overweight. Their uniforms haven't fit for years and they have the slow eyes and heavy gait of the developmentally challenged. But Tailor turns out to be right. Don't let that deceive you. They take their riot batons from their thick belts with a grace that's a thing of beauty, and once those batons are in hand, it's like watching ballet. These guys have raised a beating to the level of art. You know how George Balanchine sought a level of movement where the dance and the dancer were one? Take a lesson, Georgie-Porgie. Wherever you are, take a lesson.

Dr. Spine gets domed, but good. Then they turn on the firemen. Firemen start falling like soft rubber dolls. A fire hose swings free like a hideous hissing snake dropping anything in its path and soaking whatever is left.

Before you can say Holy-Mother-Of-Gelsie-Kirkland or Jacques d'Amboise, they've opened the skulls of the hotel manager, three of Rap's friends, and the sous chef. Then Dr. Spine gets clobbered a second time, Mona gets knocked to the ground, and Alex is about to be stomped. This pair's gone ape shit.

This one's for Rodney King. Here comes O.J. Simpson. We're way past evening the score for injustice past or present. It's indiscriminate by this point. It's a bloodbath, fourteen karat, it's over the edge. What we have here is pure institutional malice.

Then, just as the hotel is being torn to pieces, the fire hose runs out of water, the sprinklers shut off, more lights come back on, and everything gets quiet.

"That's Paris Hilton," says one of the cops.

Soon kids are saying her name beneath their breath and pleading in their hearts that she come in their direction, just so they can touch her. *Paris. Paris Hilton.* Here come the EMTs.

The way the kids are reaching out to Paris Hilton makes you remember how young they actually are. They want to touch her, make eye contact, make her part of their lives. They can't stand still, despite themselves. Neither can the firemen. Neither can the cops. Everyone is calling out

Paris Hilton's name, not out loud maybe, but they can't stop themselves from saying it. The crowd parts as if divided by the prow of a mythical ship, and for just an instant you'd swear it's the water parting, not the people.

Taylor says, "Is that who I think it is? Mom? Mom! Can you get to your feet?"

The two cops have put their batons away and made an arrest. They've handcuffed the woman from Ecuador.

More EMTs are arriving. One look at Paris Hilton and they forget why they're here. They walk away from their gurneys and shout out her name, waving their arms ecstatically.

One EMT says to me, "Do you have a pen? And something to write on?"

I tell them maybe autographs can wait. Someone needs to get Dr. Spine to a hospital. The last time I see him, Wendell Willkie is bent almost in two as she whispers into his ear. She tries to let on like she doesn't know he's sneaking looks down the front of her blouse. If she leans over much farther, he won't see anything else. Alex just looks old. We make eye contact for a second. Then she moves on, dazed and confused.

"Tell me that's not Paris Hilton," Taylor says to her brother.

"Where?"

"She's trying to get past those EMTs over there."

"Isn't this exciting," Jude says.

"Can you see her?" Taylor asks.

Jude says, "Tell me the truth, Cassie, when you were growing up in Ohio, did you ever think you'd meet Paris Hilton? Come on, let's get closer."

Taylor and Padgett make room for us. Padgett calls, "Paris. Over here."

"PARIS," cries Jude.

Padgett snaps her fingers over her head like castanets and cries, "Paris, let's dance, girl."

"Louder," says Jude. "But act like you're unimpressed."

"Don't wave, whatever you do," Tailor tells me.

Paris Hilton seems less real in person than she does when you see her on television, where she comes off as spoiled or immune. Or in photographs in magazines where her flesh can be overexploited. And the sense of reality keeps slipping as the crowd parts and she has to put one foot before the other just like everyone else. She's had to roll up her slacks so the water won't ruin them, and she's carrying her shoes in her hand, but it hasn't done much good. She's soaked before very long, which is sad. You wanted her to look like she does on TV.

She's just one more kid, lost and confused. She could be any girl here, just in the headlights of a car. As she gets closer though you can see a kind of canniness in her eyes I never expected, not intelligence exactly, just savvy, like she's gotten something for nothing and that's a heavy cross to bear. It's not exactly shame, but it's something of the sort, and it must touch a chord.

"Paris," I shout, "over *here!*"

# PART THREE

# 29 Novembar Street

## BELGRADE, 1999

On the corner a man in rags was climbing the staircase of a building. The front of the building was missing. Missing too were its roof and upper floors. Menninger watched as the man paused at each of the landings to catch his breath, resting momentarily on a balustrade, gripping the rail tightly as he forced himself to attempt the next. When he went as far as he could, he glanced about, a look of puzzlement on his face, as if someone might have been playing a very cruel prank. "You see what I mean?" said the taxi driver. "I don't put a lot of faith in these restoration plans I keep reading about. But, you never can tell. Something good might come of it yet."

That seemed unlikely, Menninger thought. You had only to look around you to recognize the state of things here. Everywhere you looked there was rubble. At best it had been pushed into heaps, the shoring of fragments against ruins, the most pitiable attempts to go on with life in a civilized fashion.

Driven from their homes at the outbreak of the fighting, people who couldn't prove they were Serbian had erected shelters for themselves amidst piles of debris. The driver said that they moved from one part of the city to another now, prodded along by a local constabulary. There were hundreds, perhaps thousands of them. Since Milosevic had withdrawn his troops from Kosovo in return for an end to the bombings, they'd become an underclass that everyone took for granted, as if it had always been in place. There was talk in the newspapers, said the driver, of the government devising a plan of some kind now that the country was officially at peace.

"Devising what?" asked Menninger.

"A plan of some kind. I wish them luck. Do you know who's out there? Croats like you, the insane, some Jews. Besides, there'll be no way to reach them. They move around too much. They're not going to trust some government windbag. Why should they, right?"

The car made a sharp U-turn in the middle of traffic and headed off in the opposite direction. "You're pale," said the driver to Menninger. A look of pity passed over the driver's face, or perhaps only an expression of ill-defined concern. The driver turned a knob on the dash and a fan began to purr. His driver was still in his teens, and in the rear of the car there was a young person's clutter, a Walkman, a T-shirt that had been used to wipe frost from the windscreen, an empty cardboard of batteries, Adidas trainers, a pair of unmatched socks that had been peeled off and forgotten, and since the fan was in the rear, the car filled with the smell of old shoes and dirty feet rather than the heat he had hoped for. Nevertheless, turning on the fan made Menninger warmer somehow. It was one of those tricks the mind plays on the body that he welcomed. The fan, the driver, the paraphernalia of ordinary living — being inside the car instead of outside there on the streets of Belgrade, the combination worked to make Menninger feel as if he were propelling himself forward toward some certain destination. They drove along the avenue for several more minutes then the driver made a series of turns.

Menninger asked what he was doing.

"You can't get through. It's blocked up ahead. Everything just stops. You have to pick it up later on. They blocked it off and established a checkpoint. You know, a gate, a guardhouse."

"What for? What are they looking for?"

"Who knows? Even they don't know, probably. It doesn't make any difference anyway. You just go around it." The car began to vibrate, as though the surface of the road had suddenly changed, as though the tires of the vehicle had completely gone out of alignment. The steering wheel shook.

At the curb, a man was bending over the fender of his automobile. The bonnet was raised and he was peering down at the engine. He rubbed his hand on his trouser leg, then reached in. A woman waited inside the car, looking around as though she'd just been harassed by a lecher and her husband had done nothing to right this. Further along, a madman working in an imaginary field threshed wheat with the swipple of his imaginary flail. Lights were just going on in some of the shop windows.

"Where should I drop you?" asked the driver.

"Anywhere," said Menninger.

"What about up there? 29 Novembar Street."

"Anywhere will do."

\*

He sat for a while in a park where paddleboats in the

shape of swans were floating in a pond. He sat on a bench and watched as children peddled them about, their paddle wheels turning and catching the light. A roasted chestnut of some sort was available from vendors, and he treated himself to a tiny paper sack of these. He chewed the nuts to their tuberculate rinds, washing them down with a syrupy, liquid concoction that came in a carton.

He was sitting and watching as well the day the internment camp was liberated. He could see cars and trucks bearing the United Nations insignia speeding around the perimeter, all headed for an area that existed beyond the walls. The conditions of the compound were abominable, the life of a Croat was worth less than a stone; still, beyond the walls, he was told, there were horrors, tortures, hideous things, unspeakable suffering.

Americans were at the wheel of the U.N. vehicles, for no particular reason that Menninger could discern, and later, meals were brought in on the trucks, on Red Cross trays, each with two cigarettes and a stick of American chewing gum. An American motion picture crew came by to make a record of this for a BBC documentary. The camera rode on the flatbed of an open truck. The truck moved slowly in a circle while production assistants walked beside it carrying muslin deflectors to increase the light. The Americans waved at the vast sea of starving Croatian captives shoveling food into their faces, trying to encourage them to smile and wave back. No one did.

Word got out that they were being released before the week was out. They weren't.

After almost a month, Menninger was taken to a building. A line extended around the building and he assumed his place at the end of it. It was late in the evening before he finally had his interview. On vacant desks, files lay about in stacks — on the desks, on the floor, in piles on vacant chairs. The officer he stood before seemed completely unembarrassed by the clutter all about.

"Come in, come in."

"Thank you," answered Menninger.

The officer looked up. "You speak English. Great. Gee. That's great. Have a seat. What did you say your name was again?"

"Albert Menninger."

The officer asked him to repeat that. Menninger repeated his name. Then the officer said, "Spell that for me, Al." Menninger did. The officer took it down on a scrap of paper, then went to the filing cabinet behind his desk and began searching through the folders. He repeated this process several times before he seemed to find what he was looking for. "Here you are, M-E-N-N-E-N" —

"Menninger," said Menninger. "I-N"

The captain was visibly discouraged. "Right, for a minute I thought we had you. I guess not though. What are you gonna do." Soon the officer gave up and returned to his desk. "What a zoo! We'll find it sooner or later. Don't worry. You're not alone. It's been like this all day. Here, let's get you started just the same."

Menninger answered the officer's questions. Family birth dates, places of birth, schooling, the years. Menninger tried to conceal the loathing he felt. The ruddy cheeks, the roll of fat around his middle, the supercilious tone he adopted, as if being overworked. How important could he be, Menninger wondered, if he were an officer doing a clerk's duty. Menninger doubted he had ever seen combat. He didn't look to be much of a fighting man. Probably something to do with a staff position at United Nations headquarters, no, not even that, just a minor aide to a minor general in some European backwater.

About halfway through the interview, the captain gave up the pretense of writing things down. He looked through his pockets then said, "You wouldn't have a match would you?"

"I don't smoke."

"I don't either. No one smokes in the States anymore. You know how many years I've been off the old coffin nails? Ten big ones." He held up ten fingers, as if speaking to a tribesman in some African jungle. "But you see what I've been seeing here —" The officer shook his head in dismay.

"I have some here in my pocket if you'd like them. They come with our meals."

The officer took the stub of a burning cigarette from the ashtray and lit a new one from its embers. "Yesterday was the worst," he began. "I was on the other side of the compound." The American shook his head to indicate disbelief. "You see something like that — Let me tell you, you never forget it. We're still not sure what went on here. The particulars. But, *ethnic cleansing*, right? We can see the results. God damn." Once again he shook his head. "My heart really goes out to you people. Believe me, I have a brand new respect. I mean it, Al, brand new."

Menninger asked when he could return home.

"That's hard to say. The best I can do right now is to get you on the first train out of here. Don't worry, I'll put you some place safe."

Safe? Yes that was the word the captain had used, *safe*.

The Americans had confused things. For all their energy and speeding about, from first stage to last, they had no idea what they were doing. What a botch they had made of things, thought Menninger. Everything in a state of utter confusion.

Jeeps broke down and they walked away and left them. Two young American corpsman carried an ancient gramophone on a litter, one of those you crank with your hand. It was playing a sentimental love song. He thought at first they were drunk, but they weren't. The simplest thing could take hours on end.

And now here he was in Belgrade, the Serbian capital, about as far away from *safe* as any Croat could be.

\*

When it began to rain, he crossed the park to the Hotel Voltaire. Apparently it had been in its day one of the better hotels in the city. The lobby was spacious. The carpet was a faded red with a faint floral pattern in gold weave. There were mirrors on the columns and gilt work up at the corbels. It had been the intention of the architect to make the room seem alight and festive, Menninger imagined, even at this time of the day, but the furniture undermined any tone of festivity. It might have been turned out locally, a Balkan rendition of what Paris might have looked like at the turn of the century.

Menninger went into its bar to warm himself with a strong drink of some kind, something to calm his stomach. Perhaps because of the early hour, the bar was virtually empty. A man and a woman sat in a dimly lit corner too far away from the bar itself for Menninger to have a look at their faces. A traveler, a man was at the other end of the bar when Menninger took a stool, but, before Menninger had time to order, he finished the last of his drink, put a few paper bills on his napkin, then left through the door just behind him.

The bartender was dressed in a waistcoat with gold epaulets. He walked past Menninger to the other end of the bar and picked up the money that had been left for him. He counted it, then held one of the bills to the light. Satisfied, apparently, he came back to the cash register and rang out the tab.

Menninger put a few bills of his own out before him. The next time the bartender was near, he said, "A whiskey, I think. A double. In a water glass."

"I'm sorry, sir. The bar's closed."

"What?"

The bartender picked up a towel and started polishing a few of the glasses that had accumulated in the sink. The man with the woman called out for a liqueur. The bartender filled a tiny glass with a thick yellow liquid, then carried it himself to the table.

"I thought you said you were closed," Menninger said to him. The bartender returned to his towel and glass. He held the glass to the light, in much the same manner as he had earlier inspected the money he'd been left.

"They were just finishing up," he said.

"Well, give me a cup of coffee then. I can see you have coffee. I'll drink it down and leave as soon as they finish their drinks."

"No coffee," said the bartender. "I've put away the last of the cups."

Several men entered the room. The tallest of the group was wearing a uniform. A city official of some sort. A policeman, perhaps, who was here on a break, away from his station. They discussed where they wanted to sit, and then, for no particular reason Menninger could make out, decided against sitting entirely. They stood together with their feet to the brass. They placed their orders and the bartender filled them.

"What's going on?" Menninger asked.

"Sir?"

"Look, I don't want any trouble. Just let me have a whiskey, all right?"

"We're all out of whiskey."

"What did you serve them then?"

"They're regular customers. They have their own private stock."

"What difference does it make whose stock it is if the bar's really closed?"

"Would you like to speak to the manager?"

"No, I'd like a glass of whiskey, please."

"Is everything copasetic down there?" asked the man in the uniform.

"Everything's fine," said the barman. "I'll tell you what," he continued, turning to Menninger. "I'll tell you where you can get a good glass of whiskey. You'll be more comfortable there. Day or night, it's always humming." He named a bar and offered Menninger directions.

For a time he walked aimlessly, ignoring the downpour. A beggar was walking along the curb in the street, picking up bits of stone and putting them in his pockets. Two stout women were talking. He remembered what his driver had said this morning about the wandering, homeless underclass and how they moved from spot to spot. He was nearing now the ravaged buildings, the debris of a highrise. He went to his left. He walked several blocks. Ahead was where he'd seen the man beneath the open bonnet of his automobile. What had his driver said about a guardhouse? Would a pedestrian be stopped there, as well as a car?

Menninger started at the sound of a voice in an alleyway. It was a woman's voice, perhaps a girl's voice, much less menacing in tone than in what it had to say: "Are you lost, or just looking for trouble?"

"Neither one," Menninger said.

"What are you looking for then?" The girl was leaning against the side of a building. One of her legs was lifted. The sole of her shoe rested flat against the brick.

"I'm not interested," Menninger said.

"How do you know?" she asked him. She had her hands inside the pockets of her coat. She opened her coat, apparently to show him the size of her breasts beneath her sweater. How old was she? The light was dim here. The rain came down in sheets. Her hair was short, he could see that much, at least. It was cut short like a boy's. That might have been the style now, here in the city. Perhaps she'd had her hair cut to make her more in vogue, more attractive to her patrons.

"You'd better bundle up," he said. He looked both ways, to the left and to the right. It was a ridiculous gesture. He was standing in the middle of a city block, yet he was looking both ways as though about to cross an intersection.

"I've never minded rain. Besides, I have a place."

"Good for you," Menninger said.

She stepped forward a pace or two and joined him on the sidewalk. Her hair was light in color. Brunette, some sort of blonde, maybe. "You don't have to sound so grumpy," she said. "I just thought you might like to see it."

"Why should I want that?"

"You're the one who's shivering from the weather, not me. I thought you might like to come inside and get warm for a while."

"I'm fine just as I am," Menninger said.

"You don't look fine. You look like you're shivering." She removed her glove and put the back of her hand to his forehead. "You may even have a little fever."

Menninger stepped forward and proceeded down the avenue. She fell into step beside him. She put her arm through his. He said, "What do you think you're doing?"

"I'm walking with you. It's a public street. I can walk here if I want."

They stopped in the middle of the next block in front of an apartment building. It was well lit, he noticed, and surprisingly respectable in appearance. There was a glass door which broached the street, then six or seven steps, then another glass door which seemed to open onto a foyer. "This is where I live," she said. She released his arm. She walked inside. He watched as she paused at the landing and retrieved her mail from a post box in the wall. She unlocked it with a key. She stood on the landing, sorting through her mail. She threw two or three pieces away in a wastebasket, then opened the next door with another key on her key ring. She held the door open with her leg as she looked through her mail more closely.

Menninger followed her into the building. They walked up two flights of stairs. She let him into her apartment. It was small, but neatly kept. One room with a kitchenette kept mostly out of view with a curtain.

She hung up her coat in a closet. She held up an envelope. "I paid this thing," she said to Menninger. She shook her head. "I paid this already. Can you believe this?"

"Why me?"

"Why not? I don't have anything against you people."

She went to the refrigerator door and opened it. She stood before the refrigerator patiently. She looked inside as though waiting for something to materialize. She then reached in and took out a bottle of milk. She opened the bottle, and brought it to her nose. Then she reached into the cupboard and took out a small glass. She held up the bottle. "Would you like some?" she asked him. "Are you hungry?"

"No thanks."

"Let's get the money out of the way before we start, okay? That way it can be fun for us both. What would you like? What should it be?"

He didn't know how to answer, for the line between flight and pursuit is forever a thin one and its margins are never well inscribed. But as he began to undress, he knew that he was crossing it, and it was as if breath was easier to draw. They might have been the first breaths he'd drawn in years, and he felt oddly at home as his eye kept coming back to her pitiful attempts to furnish the apartment beyond the bare essentials of what the country now allowed. There was a glossy eight-by-ten on the wall, held in place by a thumbtack, a middle-aged clerk's Presbyterian face, Menninger thought. A stack of bills and correspondence in a basket made of wire. Closer to him, a fluted paper cup that had earlier held a chocolate. A digital clock. A colorless overcoat made of fearnought that was hanging from the branch of a coat tree. A small jar of lip rouge that had been left on a window sill.

"Hello? What it will be?"

All he knew for sure is that it would have to disgust her.

# The Year That It Rained

Dinner came and Fanny Knatchbull ate what was put before her much as she had learned to live her life since her recent return from France. A delicate handler of all things foreign now (but certain of herself in every other way that mattered), she managed the snails without a great deal of bloodshed; only when the fish arrived served with the head *on*, and so bony was its meat and so piercing its stare that she felt prone to perform a careful, delicate tracheotomy rather than divide it into manageable bits, did Fanny nearly falter. Fortunately she picked up without hesitation and went on. She spoke with some authority when the subject of wines was raised, not once but twice as the first of these wines was poured, once in schoolgirl French, once in broken English. There were wines with each course, about which she was inevitably asked her opinion later on, this always in a way that stopped other conversations at the table, ensuring she had every other guest's attention. Here too she did well, answering each time with confidence and youthful grace, as if very old and valued accounts were now in very young and very capable hands. The white she proclaimed to be "civil" while both the Burgundy and the Bordeaux she judged "tannic," but pleasantly so, of course, after which she discussed the rain fall in Tuscany and compared it favorably with that of Bordeaux, at the same time condemning the alkaline in the soil there, linking its increase to the European Union not to mention global warming.

Her dearest friend Tom Tithall had all he could do to keep from breaking into laughter. Tom was behind all this, its instigator, and so encouraged by his gall was Fanny Knatchbull that she went on to speak of tectonic plates and saline in the water table and the impact of both on a grape's rate of growth, comparing the richness of the Burgundy's color to moral excellence in the human condition, not once, believe it or not, but twice, before someone finally thought to say, "Really? That's fascinating. But...In what sense?"

"In the sense that both a Burgundy's glow and a person's moral character are subject to all the uncertainties of nature's intervention."

"So — What you're saying then..."

"Yes, please go on — My English, it's not so good." And he did of course, for men always do of course, they never really listen to a woman, particularly when they are wearing formal clothes. So satisfied with how he'd handled his own objection was he, that by the end of what the skeptic had to say it was clear he thought Fanny was charming and graced in addition to being worldly and perceptive. In fact, so satisfied was Mr. Hired Suit here that he moved completely into Fanny's camp once the goose was on the way, yielding to necessity at the point when spears of asparagus arrived along with poached pears still in their skin, which seemed to have been arranged by Cezanne, he said, as if longing for her assurance that Cezanne was the artist who was famous for his pears, and as if Fanny, the only Parisian at the table, were singularly qualified to say.

She could not remember at all how she managed after that, but manage she did, going ahead with this ridiculous charade course by course, moving from breads to fowl to puddings in very short order, grateful to the Ritz staff at each serving for their time sense and their skills for distraction, while beaming at the other end of the table sat Tom, well into his cups by this point and just as reckless as ever, having the time of his life, even lifting his fork to her periodically to signal a toast, the sort of thing one does with those we've known and adored for as long as we can recall.

Tom had always been reckless. Even as children, Tom had been bold while Fanny had been shy, ever eager to take a leap while she'd been fearful of a fall, and in that way they'd been well-suited since they'd first begun to play. They were the only children in the neighborhood, and they'd come together by default, really. As to why they became so dear to one another, it was because of their differences, not despite them. But it was more than that as well. Neither the Tithall house nor the Knatchbull house next door was loveless exactly, or even cold; there were sunny times and warm days and occasionally pleasant if grumbling affection in both. It was just that Fanny and Tom were raised by working parents who preferred to live well beyond their means, each working several jobs to stay ahead of their creditors, and so great was the struggle to feed and educate their children in an expensive area like Coventry there wasn't energy enough for anything else.

After university, Tom changed careers with more or less the same frequency as he dry cleaned his business suits, becoming an immediate success each time, for he pushed himself relentlessly and made himself so indispensable to anyone he worked for that he became the de facto person in charge, while Fanny grew up to be a lively, light-hearted creature with hazel eyes and peach-colored skin who longed to travel. She could brighten a room with her smile. If only she'd been born with a head like Tom's, for his had been perfectly suited for school, she might have set out to be a teacher somewhere, or even better a writer, for she felt incomplete and thought there were essential lessons in the world she not only needed to learn, she needed to articulate as well; but she simply was not a book person, it simply wasn't in the cards. It was people she read with high talent, not print, some much more readily than others, Tom for instance, who she often regarded as a handsome volume with large, clear type, wide margins, and a glorious array of polished illustrations.

The first great event of life on her own was a trip through France by train that used up all of her savings. Not that she let that deter her. She went deeply in debt for a second trip to France all the same, this the following year, during which she fell in love with an unhappily married Moroccan lithographer, who later turned out be married to a woman with whom he was half-in-love at least, for he went back to his wife whom he'd sworn he'd divorce — judging from his hurried explanation and the snapshot Fanny still had, an indolent woman with mysterious eyes and ankles as thick as tree stumps and, reportedly, a passion for music.

Fanny was twenty-five by the time she moved to London, twice-traveled and now every bit the beauty Tom had predicted since they'd been fifth-formers together at Chatwell Hall; but she was cleft of heart and disillusioned with men, thinking France — like romance — was better at a distance than were it known by rail. Within the year, Tom moved to London as well, settling first in Notting Hill, where Fanny saw him regularly, and where, inevitably, Tom did most of the talking. Once a week or so Tom recounted his seeings and doings, his dining outs and business deals, while Fanny sat across from him in a dingy flat with a floor so uneven that getting to the kitchen made one appear to limp, or, alternately, forced one into a shuffle.

Later Tom moved to a better flat in the slightly less fashionable Kensington, where she couldn't report on the flooring, since she had hardly seen him at all, and then one day, out of the blue, as if they'd spoken every day for a month, Tom rang her up and said, "Fanny, welcome me back, by the way, say, can you still do that French business of yours? I want to play a joke on a friend. A dinner with an older crowd. Some fund raiser thing for my old friend Maurice. Stuffy bunch. I want you to help me teach them a lesson. Go to Paddington. I'll be there with a driver. He'll have a sign. Mademoiselle something or other. You're supposed to be my fiancée, by the way. Thing's at the Ritz, I think. Mostly foodies. I told them I was engaged to a famous Parisian gourmet. What do you say, do you have other plans? By the way, I'm leaving for Johannesburg once the evening's over, taking a taxi directly to Heathrow, so you'll have to get home on your own, I'm afraid, and if you see me picking at my food, not to worry, I never get on a flight but what I try to eat light just before."

Fanny paused before agreeing, thinking to herself that Tom was totally occupied, unique in his power to interest her, wondering to herself why she'd never been able to command Tom's attention the same proportion he clearly did hers, thinking to herself that never had he wished for her company during their childhood with the same intensity she had been wishing for his, as if pressing her hand to his heart. Tom was too old to remain so unsettled. He was inexcusable, incomprehensible, always running — like a March day — from hot fits of fever to cold, and she knew she'd be much better off if Tom found some other woman to pick up his dirty things this evening — though, truth be told, what would be the point of sending him packing when she would only go after him later on. She felt helpless to resist him. As the call ended, she agreed to drop what she was doing and be off to Paddington Station, for Fanny was still willing to attach her fate to his blindly, wholly, handsomely, no matter what Tom asked, she realized, no matter what its risks, a devotion which left her feeling as she dressed for the evening not only that women were fallible but that men were paragons of bad faith who received far better than they deserved, but also left her feeling lightheaded from the excitement that evening held in store.

Now that evening was all but over. While Tom said his goodbyes, Tom's friend Maurice, who'd been too far removed to speak to her at the table, seized the opportunity to discuss the Montrachet as he helped her with her cloak. "May I just say I love what you're wearing," he began. "So self-assured and confident. Pity the poor thing who wants the world to know all she owns so she puts it on her back. You know what I mean: All celadon and silk and strappy heels. It's always such a give-away, isn't it, when a woman's overdressed. You can tell she thinks she's a fraud."

"I should thank you all for inviting me to your lovely, elegant dinner — so quickly? Is that how it's said? My

English — I'm sorry —"

"Think nothing of it. The least we could do. And after you've come so far to be with us."

"Have I?"

"Excuse me?"

"You didn't like your Montrachet?"

His face soured. "Off year."

"Well," answered Fanny, "that was the year that it rained. No? Goodnight."

Fanny had taken a flat on Half Moon Street, across from Hyde Park, a convenient walk from the Ritz; nonetheless, Tom insisted on a taxi, explaining that a young man in a fine tux with a beautiful woman could not leave a place so grand as the Ritz *shanks mare*, as he put it. It was completely against all rules of propriety, not to mention, no doubt, the law. A taxi was not to be, however. A searchlight the size of Wales scoured the sky of the London night outside the hotel and a vintage fire engine decorated in campaign banners was parked beneath the *porte-cochère* at the hotel's entrance. Angled so it extended into the street, it succeeded in stopping traffic for several blocks. The scene was pure chaos. Horns blew and drivers shouted oaths at one another while the men who'd attended the dinner party slipped rubber gear over their evening clothes and climbed aboard, all several sheets to the wind, and this was made clear to any in doubt by those who had been issued bullhorns.

"What's all this?" Fanny asked.

"The launch of his campaign. Promised to put out fires when he put his name up. A fire truck. Get it?"

"We'll never get through," Fanny said.

Tom took her hand. "This way. We'll manage."

Fanny found herself as women in heels often find when they are walking with their escort, for she was struggling to keep up with Tom as if she were the younger sister and Tom her older brother, for she tried to keep pace with his stride while he did nothing to adjust his to hers. They walked this way in silence until Fanny sighed to herself, then she blurted out the story of her Moroccan lithographer, in copious — even painstaking — detail, sparing Tom nothing and making up a few things whole cloth to ensure that her story would be as shocking to Tom as it had come to seem to her. "Do you see, Tom?"

"Yes. That is, I think so."

Meaning to lighten Fanny's mood, but having no idea whatsoever as to how he should respond to what she just told him (but pathetically eager to please nonetheless, as men often are in such circumstances, since they naturally assume a woman is fishing for a compliment when all she really wants after being jilted is to find a man, virtually any man, who will accept her definition of who she is and why), Tom remarked, "You were wonderful tonight, Fan. The envy of every woman, the desire of every man."

"Really? I wasn't a bore? You're certain?"

"Oh no. The farthest thing from it."

"What was all that anyway?"

"Bunch of Euro swine, think they know something about grub. Seems the previous candidate they backed spoke superficially of soup and they dropped him like a rock."

"I'm sorry?"

"Trying to raise money for some sort of political campaign or other, don't ask me why, can't hope to win, poor

Maurice, can he? I mean, a fire engine. Seriously."

"Ah, Maurice. Yes. Maurice."

"My friend, you met him, you were seated cater-cornered. A fund raising thing. A million pounds a plate or something — I told him I could produce this famous French — Really? I didn't tell you any of this in advance?"

Putting his arm around her shoulder and drawing her near, Tom added, "You don't know how I've missed you, Fanny Knatchbull. Are you seeing someone new? After this lithographer, I mean."

"Someone unprincipled."

Tom responded that he couldn't be happier for her then, since Jane Austin's warnings aside, a woman would be foolish not to align herself with an unprincipled man when it's clear to any girl — and certainly any young woman — that it's unprincipled men with whom life is truly a pleasure, and, conversely, a principled life with someone attentive and wholesome and civil is precisely what drives women to drink and despair.

"I meant you, silly. This evening. We're engaged, Tom, remember?"

"In that case," said Tom, "I demand a kiss." Tom swept her up in his arms and bent her backwards in some ridiculous version of a Hollywood swoon circa 1940, where eyes meet and lights dim to the swell of fine violins.

"You're awful," Fanny giggled.

"Yes, I am, guilty as charged."

"Well? Are you going to stand me up?"

"Not until I've done this." Tom kissed her. Playfully at first, she thought. Then not. And then, as if she were discovering in herself a tiny engine increasing to a throb, she was kissing too, surrendering herself to the moment as if being lowered toward the fiery pits of Hell, reasoning this could not be an earthly pleasure, it was far too grand from the get-go.

"There," said Tom stiffly, putting Fanny back on her feet.

"You've had your kiss, Tom."

"Brilliant, right, I have, haven't I?"

If only one of them, for even a moment, might have found in the kiss the least hint of ambiguity! If theirs had only been, say, a physical sensation alone, Tom might have known what to do. But no. Feeling the flutter of her heart, the beat of Fanny's heart in hand, then the beat of his own, Tom saw the moment in the naked light of truth and was startled by it, meat, bone, and marrow.

Fanny said, "It's getting cold, Tom. Let's cross to the other side of the park."

"Why don't we?"

"What's taking you to South Africa?"

"Banking."

"Oh anything but that."

"I'm afraid so. Dreary, isn't it. Who knows what could have been going through my mind."

"Goodness. *Pauvre petite.*"

They walked on, creating a silence now so loud it approached the point of deafening them both. Fanny knew what he was thinking, for she was thinking it too, but she could see in his eyes that Tom was desperate for her to sidestep the subject, so Fanny remarked on a young woman she knew Tom had been seeing, a girl she knew to be a fortune hunter, and so promptly did Tom rise to this young woman's defense that Fanny assumed from his tone she'd confused this young woman with another, until she understood he was teasing again. He was explaining the girl's behavior by proposing that since the girl in question had been raised as a Quaker she had been taught that all men were equal under the eyes of God, no matter their race or culture or predilections, and hence all should be treated as one, with the many no more or less discriminated than the few, so if she was pursuing Tom because he had been doing very well for himself economically, it was because she saw no reason — at least in matters of the heart — to hold his good fortune against him. If anything, she embraced his present economic state and wished him all the best in this regard for the future, and if at some point ahead he became very rich indeed, then she would feel it was God's will that she look past his luscious millions and love him only for himself.

"Which is jut as the Creator intended, I haven't a doubt," said Fanny.

"Nor I."

"You mount a powerful defense, Tom."

"I do, don't I, I rise to the occasion."

"Almost every time."

"What was it your father used to say?"

"Despots bring about the servant class, but then servility brings about despots?"

"No. I was thinking of something else: 'A polite kiss is Pity's sister' — Not to put too fine a point on it, Fan, but I might have had too much wine with my dinner."

"From the look of your shirt, I'd say you got most of it *on you* and not *in you*."

"Oh God. So I did. I can't wear this on a plane. And

I've packed all the others. Maybe we should go somewhere and try to see to it. Club soda or something."

"There's always my place."

"Well, if it's on the way. Then later I'll get a taxi."

"Yes," said Fanny, linking their arms. "Let's."

Surprisingly, now that one of them had been brave enough to address the kiss in conversation, she felt none of Tom's need to revise the moment. She'd been as surprised as he was, but once the kiss began she knew what any woman knows who has been kissed for the first time by the man she was meant to be with, namely, that she has but one real prospect for happiness and the man she's just kissed *is* that prospect, and surprisingly, perhaps amazingly, for the first time in her life Fanny felt both tutored and complete.

Tom asked, "Which flat is yours, Fan?"

"Over there. We'll have to cross to the light."

"Show me again."

"There. See the Athenaeum Hotel? Follow it to the end. You see that lane? No, look up the street, toward Starbucks."

"Let me see where you're pointing."

"On the corner, the light in the window?"

For a moment she thought Tom meant to kiss her again. Tom paused. She paused. He put his cheek alongside her own as if to follow where she was pointing, then just as quickly removed it. A look of great distress flashed across his face. He was waiting for her to reassure him, she could see, to tell him what were they were about to do was perfectly fine, would work out perfectly well. Fanny had no idea why that mattered, not in the greater scheme of things. To her, they had already crossed the line, a line the size of a gulf, not a fissure, a gulf that had already separated them from what they had meant to one another lo these many years, while to Tom, well, there's nothing half so frightening to a young man as sleeping with a woman he actually loves. Tom was looking at her like a little boy. He was looking at her as if just a moment before everything in his life had been perfectly fine, and she had ruined it out of malice.

"Right, Good, Well. You've taken a room in Ferndean Manor then," Tom continued. "Who lives above you, not a madwoman in an attic, I trust."

"It's really not that bad."

"Don't let her near matches is all."

"Stop it. Now you're just being a snob. It's not very large, but it's reasonably comfortable. Wait till you see it inside before you pass judgment."

"Perhaps we ought to hurry."

Fanny replied, "Sorry, Tom, I'm in heels."

"Was that a drop of rain I just felt?" asked Tom.

"What *is* that? Up there?"

They both turned their heads toward Green Corner at the sounds of a terrible ruckus. A siren was bleating into the London damp as if gasping for its last breaths of air while a rotating blue lamp pulsed, then stuttered. Fanny recognized the truck before Tom did. She remembered the E R F on its grill and how the letters had sparkled beneath the *porte-cochère*. The truck was an ancient Water Tender marked as having belonged to the Tynemouth Fire Brigade years earlier, and the drunken revelers had managed to start the pumps and get one of the fire hoses working. They were sitting in a row on its top like a crew deadset on winning a longstanding tug of war, each of them holding onto a section of the hose as it jerked and swayed. A steep arc of water shot miles into the air then traced a path forward as the truck moved on, soaking all its path, while the drunks did their best to keep from falling off the truck and breaking their fool necks. One of them spotted Tom from afar and began calling out his name, encouraging him to join them. As the driver slowed the truck to a crawl, another shouted, "You look like a mad dog just bit you in the foot, Tithall. Get up here where you belong."

"Well don't just stand there like a damned fool. Come on," shouted another.

"Fanny?" asked Tom. "I don't think I have much choice."

"Come on, Tithall," shouted the driver, "we don't have all night."

Tom turned to Fanny and said, "Are you sure you'll be all right from here?"

The truck began to pull off without Tom, primarily because the driver was seeing double and couldn't feel the brake pedal beneath his foot, Fanny imagined, but it wasn't long before a hundred hands reached out in Tom's direction. He had to run to climb aboard, but climb aboard he did, taking his place alongside those clinging to the trunion bars. A bell clanged in his honor. A light, portable auxiliary pump came unmoored when its stainless steel clamp rings loosened, so someone kicked it free and it went rolling off on its own. Then the truck jumped a kerb and as it gained speed nearly ran down two Hyde Park pedestrians before setting off across the wide, wet lawns toward the trees, its engine sputtering. Everyone was so drunk they didn't notice. Shouts were coming through the bullhorns as the truck moved toward the trees, its engine dead now, overturning benches and sideswiping trash bins. Fanny tried to make out Tom from the others, most of them distant and greedy, slickered, brutal, and brilliant in the moonlight, for such is how men seem to someone Fanny's age, and at last she did, just as the truck passed over a knoll toward the tree line. Tom had made his way toward the ladder hand over fist and was hanging now from its end as if swaying from a trapeze.

Then the light changed and Fanny hurried across the intersection as women do when wearing ridiculously uncomfortable shoes, as if feet rather than shoes were surely the nuisance.

## A Reversal of His Fortunes

Muybridge turned up his collar against the chilly London rain. It was every bit a downpour, and he was thinking to himself as he soaked to the skin that there were better ways for a man to make a living than the line he was in. He tugged at the brim of his Donnegal hat until its short brim fully covered his ears. Damn their eyes anyway, the blue bloods just loved playing spy, Muybridge thought. It might as well have been their national pastime.

He was on his way to meet Lord Anthelm at the lord's private club for a five p.m. supper. To Muybridge's amusement, the lord was one of those *very British* characters who took themselves more seriously than they really had a right to, and Muybridge might have been more eager to keep the engagement were its occasion only social, for Lord Anthelm was widely recognized as a lithe conversationalist as well as a raconteur with many a story to tell of his derring-do amidst webs of intrigue. Muybridge understood he had been a high ranking official of MI-5, Britain's legendary intelligence branch. The lord had never put this behind him, apparently, and he was a character in other ways as well. The first impression he'd made on Muybridge was of someone who would have been more at ease in trunk hose and a doublet than the bowler he always wore or his Saville Row tailoring, and the image — somehow — stuck. Lord Anthelm had impressed him upon a first meeting as an amusing, patrician fop who was a thousand years removed from his proper place in history, and Muybridge had yet to shake this impression. He might add to it, as he sometimes had in the past two years, having discovered over time that the lord was always freshly shaven, polished, well spoken, ready to pay what he owed, even throw in a bonus. He might take away from it, thinking, as he was thinking at the instant, that the man was a pain in the rectum. But what came to mind first each time the lord wished to contract for his services was of doublets and trunk hose, so fully had this colored his view of the man from the get-go.

Muybridge had been told to be at the intersection of Kensington Road and Bright Lane at precisely a quarter past the hour, only if it continued to rain. He was to stand on the northeast corner, per usual, where a taxi would stop. When he was asked where he wished to be taken, he was to say, "Not fit weather for ducks. I'm soaked through and through. Forgot my umbrella. A silly thing to do." He had been given as well a bushel of particulars, the registration number of the driver, something about a scarf to be found on the left side of the taxi that had been purposely placed to appear to have been lost in a rush. More. Muybridge really couldn't bother.

His rendezvous with the taxi was five minutes off, there was no scarf, but, so wet, so frozen to the bone, his identifying words rang as true as any shibboleth in the history of man. So too did the response of the driver. The engine stalled as he pulled away from the kerb. Pumping the accelerator, he said, "Nasty little car. Can't keep it started. Must be the choke. And didn't I just have it worked on? I've got the receipt somewhere. Is something the matter?"

After being driven around London for the better part of

an hour, Muybridge was let off at the point from which his tour had begun, Bright Lane and Kensington Road, though on the opposite side of the street. Muybridge waited for traffic to lighten before making his way across to a broken-down four-door. This car was badly parked at the northeast corner several feet into the street and at an angle to the kerb, an ancient yellow Ford, on its right fender a crimp several inches deep. Its bonnet was up. Muybridge positioned himself beside it. He set foot off the kerb, looked up and down the block impatiently, as if hoping for assistance. The car, from all appearances, was his. A second taxi, identical to the one he had recently suffered a ride in but not— of course — the same one at all, stopped. Muybridge opened its door, ducking his head as he climbed inside. He said, "Nasty little car. Can't keep it started. Must be the choke. And didn't I just have it worked on? I've got a receipt somewhere. Is something the matter?"

Meeting Muybridge's eyes in his rearview mirror, the driver responded, "A gentleman friend of mine just cut his throat upon a beach."

They drove a circuitous route that led them past the Academy of St. Martin's in the Fields several times repeatedly, each at a different speed. Convinced that they had not been followed, the driver turned down a lane that few even knew existed, and near the end of that lane he deposited his passenger.

Muybridge entered the building with minutes to spare before his five p.m. supper and he used this time to enjoy his surroundings. The club was not overly large, nor were there many rooms, but all of its appointments were striking to the eye, and no doubt authentic. Lord Anthelm had once said in passing that he no longer attended state banquets because they'd been reduced to the level of a catered affair for conventioneers. Neither would he dine at Buckingham Palace. No longer was there a display of *objets d'art*, he said, no personal belongings, nothing from the Royal gardens since even the flowers were provided by florists he had no respect for, a chain of flower shops actually controlled by Rupert Murdock, the Australian. For fear of souvenir hunters, anything apart from the Royals daily life was carefully removed hours in advance an event. "Not so much as a show of plate!" No, it was not, he thought, as such clubs went, what one might have expected these days, neither some Ralph Lauren facsimile of faded Windsor grandeur nor some smoky male retreat. No roaring fire or worn leather sofas or the whiff of a cricket pitch. No polished dark paneling, nor a mustachioed masculine aura. The farthest thing from them, he dared say.

Muybridge passed through a foyer where silk tapestries hung from the walls at intervals. Near a cloakroom, there was a Regency mirror of carved wood inlaid with plates of pounded silver that had been rubbed to a high, fine finish. Muybridge deposited his very damp trench coat and hat with an ancient attendant, then proceeded toward the anteroom where he usually met his host. Feeling feverish and chilled, Muybridge rubbed his hands together as he waited, as if warming them over an open fire.

A banquet was being arranged in a room set aside for that purpose alone. Its double doors were temporarily open. He'd dined here twice before and they'd always been locked — he knew, he'd tried them, making him more curious than ever about what those doors concealed. It was symptomatic of how men like Muybridge lived their lives, for there was nothing half so inviting as a door that was locked to him, save, perhaps, a locked door that was suddenly open. Too, he had years of practice to draw upon. Insinuating yourself into places you didn't belong was a necessary skill to those who murdered strangers for a livelihood.

The banquet room was not large and since two grand pianos were arranged side by side, it seemed smaller than it needed to be, making the servicing of twelve dinner guests a cross between plans for a landing at Normandy and the fussy choreography of the Bolshoi Ballet, he imagined. Muybridge looked up at the walls. Ornate appointments. Far too self-involved. His eyes surveyed the ceiling, brushing them in a way that was so light yet tactile he might have been running the edge of his thumb across the edge of a very sharp razor. He had no taste for the room's tortuous curves. No, it was nothing he'd choose for himself, not even if such places were actually available to people like Muybridge, which of course they'd never be. But the banquet room was no less impressive for that. A serving staff was now moving in and out of the room, preparing the table for the evening ahead. The plates to be found beneath the covers were its sole decoration for the moment. Even so, he thought, they were precisely arranged in a row so straight it might have been measured in millimeters with those tiny blue flexible rulers, which, in fact, he had no doubt had been the case. Lord Anthelm had explained the club's formal dinner service had come from the Duke of Windsor's estate. They been made for the court of Catherine the Great by a direct descendant of Josiah Wedgwood at the Wedgwood factory in Chelsea, Stratfordshire, each plate depicting a famous event from Greek mythology, and each of the covers bore the crest of a different royal family from the roary-glory days of Europe. An amusing thought passed through Muybridge's mind: In at least one of the plates was he apt to find a crack? As he was about to see for himself, Lord Anthelm, appearing as suddenly as if he'd appeared from the woodwork, said, "There you are, Muybridge, how good of you to come. I thought perhaps we'd lost you. Why didn't you show yourself to our table?"

Right, thought Muybridge. He would not, of course, have been welcome in any of the dining areas without the presence of his host here. He would have been shooed away like a stray dog had he gone it alone. "Good evening, Lord Anthelm," said Muybridge, extending his hand. Rather than take his hand, Lord Anthelm steered him back to the vestibule by the elbow, which was more in keeping, he meant Muybridge to realize, with where Muybridge belonged.

Muybridge said, "There seems to be a banquet in the works for this evening, Lord Anthelm."

He wanted to add, in whose honor is it being held, Bismarck's? Napoleon's? Fredrick the Great's? A little shindig for the Hapsburgs perhaps? Looking down the narrow hallway through which he was now being led, it would not have surprised Muybridge to find a row of pages lined up against the walls in white satin knee britches and satin waist coats with bullion embroidery, each boy with his own powdered wig and a sword in an enameled scabbard.

Lord Anthelm seemed to have guessed what was going through Muybridge's mind from the expression that crossed his face momentarily, and he was not about to allow Muybridge the pleasures of social inferiority. Their meeting, apparently, had already begun.

"What, oh that?" said Lord Anthelm. "Just a small dinner party actually. The members are bringing their wives. A few convivial friends who have nowhere else to wear their formal clothes. No one dresses for dinner anymore, you see. Not even in the city's best restaurants. You're mistaken for a *maître d'* if you so much much as dare to. It's more for the wives than the members actually. They need a place where they can show off their baubles without feeling conspicuous. Being well-heeled has become the cultural equivalent of the eighth deadly sin. Here, no one really bothers. You'd be surprised how hard it is to recruit a younger membership. We show them around and you'd think we were Madame Tussaud's. And for all I know, we actually are. What to my generation was simply a part of *l'art de vivre* has gone by the way, apparently. Suppose it can't be helped. All depends on how you look at it, doesn't it. One generation's era of *l'art de vivre* becomes the *époque de mauvais goût* of the next?"

When they were seated at a table for two by a steward, Lord Anthelm got right to the point. "I'm told there's a problem. I handpicked you, you realize, Muybridge. You recognize, of course, you're putting egg all over my face?"

Muybridge removed his serviette from a solid sterling collar. "That wasn't my intention. I want to know more about what I'm getting myself into, that's all. I've come to you before. You've heard me out. We've talked."

Lord Anthelm took his linen serviette from the plate before him and spread it neatly across his lap, smoothing its edges as he spoke. "These new heads, Muybridge, they haven't appreciation enough for practical politics, *Realpolitik*, as it was called in my day. So many of these chaps I run into

171

imagine differences of opinions among longstanding enemies can simply be jawboned away. No sense of bad blood, of how deeply it runs. Too much faith in the wizardry of words."

Muybridge said, "Too little stomach for what needs to be done."

"Precisely," said Lord Anthelm.

So at least they had that much out of the way, thought Muybridge. Someone, somewhere, would have to be assassinated in the immediate future, someone known to them both probably, and the risk of failure was steeper than the norm. Thank God it was on the table. He'd been afraid in the taxi this might drag on for hours, late into the night.

Lord Anthelm continued, "All the pleasures of a job well done come from the felicity of the way they phrase things, you see. We've raised a full generation of talkers. Talkers, not doers, as the Americans like to put it."

Muybridge had been reared in Leicestershire, but he was Canadian by birth and he was never certain when Lord Anthelm mocked Americans this way if he was being taken into the man's confidence or being tested to see if he was keen-witted enough to recognize the snub. Muybridge smiled graciously in any case, thinking to himself that there'd been something contemptuous in Lord Anthelm's tone since he'd discovered Muybridge in the banquet room.

Lord Anthelm raised his hand. Beckoning for the waiter, Muybridge imagined in passing. Menus, he supposed. Then, as if Muybridge had spoken those words aloud without realizing it, Lord Anthelm said, "I took the liberty of ordering in advance for the two of us, I hope you won't mind. Proscuitto and melon. It's one of the advantages to dining here as opposed to a restaurant, ordering off menu, I mean. What's left over from lunch isn't being touted as fresh by some insolent waiter who was only last week a zinc miner in the north."

He debated with Muybridge the merits of two French wines, both of them white, apparently, one of them fruitier than the other, while the *sommelier* looked on, as of yet unacknowledged. The actual debate was between the *sommelier* and his host, Muybridge warranted, for later Lord Anthelm deferred to the *sommelier* who suggested a red alternative when the final choice was left in his hands, a French Bordeaux, a 1981 Chateau Mouton Rothschild, a suggestion he made in a diffident voice.

As the *sommelier* disappeared to the wine cellar, Lord Anthelm resumed their conversation from an earlier point as if nothing had interceded. "Talkers, Muybridge. Not doers. Not men like ourselves. You've distinguished yourself to me, I hope you realize that."

"Distinguished myself how?"

Muybridge waited for Lord Anthelm to continue. Had his host been a woman rather than a man, Muybridge might have anticipated a brush of her hand against his own right about now, or to have his knee touched in some cloying, intimate fashion. A gesture meant to warm him up, not arouse him of course. *That* would come later.

"Tell me something, Muybridge. What keeps you at this? It can't be the money. What is it, the intrigue?"

"It's what I do best."

"It's a matter of self-respect then."

"Not at all. I'm against self-respect, and in all of its forms."

Had he been wearing them, Lord Anthelm might have

been looking at Muybridge over the top of his demi-lune spectacles, the ones he sometimes wore for reading. "You realize, finding myself in a tight spot, I could have turned to anyone. I chose you in particular. I like to think we understand each other. In fact, I like to think we're cut from much the same cloth."

"You flatter me, Lord Anthelm."

"I understand the ways of my world."

"You've established a reputation for yourself in these matters that will never be equaled, at least not in your lifetime."

"Now who's flattering whom, Muybridge. Come, come, *Ne penche pas le chapeau por moi.*"

So that was it, thought Muybridge. A tight spot, was it? It wasn't Muybridge who had distinguished himself from a vast cache of readily available independent contractors. It was the assignment itself that was different. That was not a good sign. What was that expression about the hairs rising on the back of one's neck as an instinctive response to some imminent danger? His own stayed put. But he understood the figure of speech. He had a very good sense of the dicey situation. It was every bit a necessity in his line of work.

Two goblets were placed before them by a boy in his teens in an ill-fitting tuxedo shirt too wide at the collar. The *sommelier* returned with the bottle of Bordeaux. Lord Anthelm offered Muybridge the honors, which he was expected to refuse. So expected, he refused and watched with feigned interest the hollow ritual that followed.

He looked at Lord Anthelm across the rim of his glass as he awaited the pour. Yes, thought Muybridge, he wasn't far off the mark, an Arthurian knight. An old knight errant on a grail quest. But no reason to underestimate him. Couldn't assume a Don Quixote. Less quixotic, less comic. A knight wandering on foot through a waste land. Yes, that was closer to it. And having slaughtered his horse for food, there was nothing to do now but look back at its bony remains as he came to terms with starving to death himself or dying of exposure. Muybridge said, "I've been thinking of getting out of the business, actually. I'm beginning to lose my nerve, I think."

"That's an important consideration," Lord Anthelm replied. "A golfer addressing his ball on a tee who wonders if he may hit into the foursome ahead of him isn't ready to hit a good drive, is he? It makes no difference if the foursome in the distance is well beyond his normal range. When the last thought in his mind is a fear of hitting too long, he's sure to pull off in some manner. Step back, is my advice to him. Let his partner tee off instead, even if out of turn. You golf, I imagine, Muybridge?"

"Not for many years. And not well when I played."

"Quite so. That's reason enough right there to give up the game. If you can't do it well, why do it at all?"

Their meals were brought to the table, identical plates of carefully ripened melon and stingy strips of Italian ham. At once gracious but brusque, Lord Anthelm had mastered the art of dealing with servants. He dispatched their servers with nary a thought to their presence, then spoke with a first bite of food in his mouth. "It seems to me that there needs to be a display of some minimal level of skill before they allow a golfer to have access to the links. He can ruin things for everyone, if the poor dear's a duffer. Always off in the rough. His foursome there as well, looking for his ball. What fun is that? — Try your prosciutto, Muybridge. Mine's damnably tasty. Is yours as well?"

"It's golf we're discussing now? Not anything else? I wouldn't think my level of skill would be a matter of contention."

"Oh, my dear boy, it's not. I'm trying to say I'm in complete agreement, that's the point I'm carrying home. Nerves, you see. That's the point I'm making. They can get the best of any of us."

They ate a few bites apiece before continuing their talk. Neither seemed to have brought much of an appetite to the table. Still, eating a meal was all part of a thin, social veneer that might set the stage for the real occasion of their meeting. Muybridge was conscious of the sounds of their cutlery, its clank against the china. While it was a familiar charade, something about it this evening had begun to make him uneasy. It seemed effeminate, somehow. They were playing with their suppers as two little girls might have pretended a tea.

It was common practice to work out the terms of an assassination well before its target was indicated. A name was never proffered before all the terms were settled; it simply wasn't done, at least not among professionals. This was more than common practice. More, too, than good form. Such procedures had about them a kind of elegance that kept the grimy business at hand from soiling one's fingers, and with that in mind, Muybridge made a show of appreciating his surroundings, which were elegant to the detail. The dining room was smaller than he'd remembered, but it might well have been a room in a palace nonetheless. It had an arched, painted ceiling with its coffered gilt-work done in high relief. Beautiful chandeliers, cut rock crystal, Muybridge assumed, which reflected the light, light that reflected yet again from the molding, for a molding of uninterrupted Regency gold separated the wall from the ceiling and helped to define the room's shape. Each wall with its carved pilaster, each with its own hand-painted murals representing the four quarters of the world.

"What do you think, Muybridge, too flouncy? Are you a Bauhaus man? I imagine you are. A taste for basic shapes and simple lines."

"No, it's not to my taste, actually. Impressive, nevertheless."

"It's not to my taste either, my boy."

Lord Anthelm made Muybridge uneasy. "Really? I'm surprised."

"It's always seemed to me that the style is, well, too much ado about not quite enough. If you see what I mean."

They weren't talking about the décor of the room of course. They were talking about the negotiations that still lay ahead, and it was as if he was giving up too easily what he thought he needed least, it seemed to Muybridge. Lord Anthelm knew how the game was suppose to be played. Agreeing to renegotiate this way was like sacrificing a pawn in a chess game. You had to arrange your pieces far in advance and make the vulnerable pawn seem nothing but an oversight. He would have preferred Lord Anthelm kept reminding him that he wasn't British by birth, insulting him. He was in much too big a hurry, Lord Anthelm. Or careless. Or worse, contemptuous of Muybridge, condescending. Yes, that was more likely. But maybe it was something else entirely, something new.

For the first time since Muybridge had met him, Lord Anthelm seemed to be showing the ill-effect of his age. Muybridge kept expecting to detect a tremor of his hand, a slight palsy of the head. Something. Lord Anthelm seemed to be dealing from a position of weakness rather than strength, from shopworn wisdom instead of virility. A desperation he was unaccustomed to seeing across the table. If so, that was worse. Muybridge did not do business with desperate men. Not if he could help it. At least he did not do business with desperate men unless he was very well compensated for the additional risk this entailed to his life and well-being.

Muybridge decided upon a ploy. He would ask to be told who was to be assassinated before a money amount was agreed upon. Insofar as Lord Anthelm stood his ground, they might yet be in business. If he capitulated and offered the name though, the evening was finished. Find the back door. Metaphorically speaking, leave by the fire escape. Lord Anthelm would have to be very desperate indeed if he gave him the name, that always came from someone else. That would be tantamount to contracting for the murder himself. No, Muybridge did not do business with desperate men if there was any good way to avoid it, particularly those who fancied themselves as being honorable men, as did Lord Anthelm. Those were the worst of all. If they found your wallet stuffed with pound notes between the cushions of their sofa, they would drive hell to leather in order to return it, refusing to rest until they saw it in your hand again. While at your cottage, however, if they lost a sixpence bet, they would sooner leave England than pay you what was yours.

"I was wondering, Muybridge, do we amuse you, the old

uppercrust, I mean? I was watching your face as you were looking around the room, you see. Quite all right if we do. We amuse the Americans, I know. They think we're quaint. Something straight out of Austen or Thomas Hardy. Or something off of their Tele, the educational channels. I won't take offense, I swear."

There was that mocking tone again. "*Interest me*, perhaps. Not amuse me. I was wondering earlier who would be attending that banquet I saw being set as I arrived, for instance."

Cutting the last of a strip of prosciutto, Lord Anthelm answered, "A duke. A duchess. Your odd baronet. No one very remarkable, really."

Lord Anthelm signaled for coffees.

Who, Muybridge wondered, would have to be murdered? That's what he wanted to know next. It would be in keeping with what he knew of Lord Anthelm for the man to shift the blame for some snafu to someone else, then have that person killed. He was subject to mistakes now that he was aging, and he was not above being a scurrilous coward, not when it came to a cock-up. Kill or be killed. Eat or be eaten. One of the higher-ups, Muybridge guessed. Something internal to British Intelligence. Tag, you're it! Bang, you're dead!! Yes, that was one alternative, certainly.

Muybridge pushed his plate forward, placing his cutlery atop his melon in the shape of an X. "Where, precisely, do I fit into all this, Lord Anthelm?"

"As you suspect. As always."

"Who?"

Their coffees were set before them by a ginger-haired waiter. Once he was gone, Lord Anthelm said, "Something wrong with your melon, was there?"

"Mine was green."

"Mine too, actually."

"This time I want to know in advance."

"I want many things. It's the cross we must bear for our sins."

Lord Anthelm stirred at his coffee with at a tiny sterling spoon, held delicately between his forefinger and thumb. Still stirring his coffee to cool it, Lord Anthelm made what amounted to a particularly attractive financial offer without naming a precise figure, though, had the offer been tape-recorded, there was no way to prove that. Had the offer been made in any other form, Muybridge would have left the table and walked straight out the door, never to have contact with Lord Anthelm again. "That's our *final* offer, by the by, though I'm confident you'll find this very generous indeed," said Lord Anthelm.

"I find in myself a kind of impatience which I don't seem to be able to help. I think I'm losing my taste for the way I make my living."

"Impatience breeds carelessness. None of us can afford to be careless. Not in this day and age. Not in any line of work. There are too many pitfalls. What is true for you and me is true for everyone else, simply less so."

"I feel as if I'm waiting on queue for a dowager hunting change in her coin purse. I know when I see her begin counting out her coins that she won't get it right the first time. If impatience breeds carelessness, do you suppose experience breeds impatience?"

"What can I do?"

"Actually, I've been thinking of a change of scenery. I've

been thinking about a holiday."

Lord Anthelm assumed, obviously, that Muybridge was testing the waters for gold. And, in fact, when Muybridge demanded to see him this evening, money *was* precisely what he had in mind, not background information. But everything about this evening was putting Muybridge on edge. If he was being asked to kill one of their own, the risks he faced could prove daunting. It had to do with those hairs on the back of his neck that should have stood up, but didn't.

"Anywhere in particular, Muybridge?" He took a drink of his coffee. From his expression, it was tepid. "A restorative walking tour in the Lake Country, is it, Muybridge? A chance to clear your cluttered mind by taking in some of England's natural wonders? Would that put your weary mind to rest?"

Muybridge hated being mocked. He reached across the table and grabbed Lord Anthelm by the wrist. "What would put my mind at rest is to learn who you want killed, and how you want it done."

Through gritted teeth, Lord Anthelm said, "Release me, you fool. Most men in my position would not have dared meet with you this evening at all."

The steward who had greeted them as they entered the dining room upon their arrival appeared at their table. "Is everything to your satisfaction, Lord Anthelm?" he asked. Lord Anthelm looked at Muybridge. Muybridge released him.

"Very well, thank you. Top-hole, the melon this evening."

Lord Anthelm seemed shaken by the way he'd been man-handled. Poor bastard looked to be on the very point of apoplexy, thought Muybridge, trying to stifle a smile. He'd have to be more careful next time, Muybridge reminded himself. He'd meant to jar the man a little, not send him to his grave. Lord Anthelm was rubbing his wrist like someone who'd felt their capillaries swell at the onset of a stroke.

"I'm very pleased to hear that, Lord Anthelm," said the steward. He returned to his duties.

Lord Anthelm said, "I'm simply trying to clarify my position."

"You've made yourself clear enough. I want time to think this over, Lord Anthelm. I want to be certain of what I'm getting myself into."

"I can't do that. Events are already underway. Things have to go forward." He finished his coffee, then adopted an avuncular tone, a Dutch uncle offering a lesson. He said, "Don't do anything you'll live to regret. Sleep on it. Wipe the slate clean. Both of us. We'll be in contact again tomorrow. I can give you a few hours. A few days? That's out of the question."

"I'll need tomorrow."

Lord Anthelm continued, "I can give you until tomorrow night. Here again? You owe me that. You owe me that much, and more."

"The same drill?" said Muybridge, pushing himself away from the table.

"We can eliminate the taxis if you like. I know that gets on your nerves."

A few years ago Lord Anthelm would have never allowed himself to be manipulated into such a hopeless bargaining position. He was simply too old for this now, Lord Anthelm. He'd passed the point of effectiveness. A reversal of fortunes. The first sign of a man who suffers a reversal of fortunes is the inability to know when it's time to get out. Muybridge was not looking forward to the aging process himself. Muybridge was reaching the stage of life where he needed to be taking better care of his body.

Lord Anthelm continued, "Indulge me, my boy. A man of my years has so few pleasures left. What's a little inconvenience?"

Lord Anthelm rose. Taking him by the elbow, Lord Anthelm said, "You're not like all the others. big eyed ideologues. Ersatz soldiers of fortune still wet behind the ears. Some of the chaps I meet are sociopaths, better off behind bars. What passes for spirit in the others is often breathtaking audacity instead. You're singularly impressive. I feel by now as if we've established a rapport, working together as we have. I like to think we understand one another. That we can trust one another."

The door at the end of the hall opened onto a service lane. At the end of the lane, to his left, Muybridge could see a blue canvas *porte-cochère* beyond which his taxi would soon await him. Lord Anthelm said something to the effect that the rain had finally stopped, thank goodness, dreadful business all these windy storms, which reminded Muybridge that he had forgotten his trench coat and rain hat. "Isn't that always the way," said Lord Anthelm. "I've done the same thing myself here, I don't know how many times. Never you worry, dear boy. You go ahead. I'll get your things. It's the least I can do."

Muybridge was relieved to be outside. Alone. He'd recently given up cigarettes, and he longed for one at the moment. He thought of dragging the smoke into the lining of his lungs with devastating force. The memory itself was salivary. Lord Anthelm seemed to deflate before his eyes, he thought, pleading his case in that desperate, teary tone. He was afraid the old fool was about to kiss him on both cheeks. Had he heard correctly? An offer to ring him up in the morning? Lord Anthelm was slipping. It was an amusing image. Palms moist, listening for a call that, of course, wasn't coming. Well let him sit there and tremble in exasperation. A dash of humility might do him some good. Give him a taste of what the rest of us go through. The poor bastard was over the hill, wasn't he? That was the problem with the blue bloods. In a game of cat and mouse, they took it for granted that they were the felines. All gamesmanship now. All process. You couldn't survive in their world once you lost your passion for evil, and Muybridge made a note: that dulled the nerves, that diluted the juices.

The rain had ceased. He took a deep breath. The air was nippy, even bracing, one might say. The dining room, he now realized, had been unbearably stuffy. In fact, that's the last thought he had, those very words, *unbearably stuffy*.

Before he realized what was happening, Lord Anthelm had come upon him from the rear. He'd slit his throat from ear to ear with a pearl handled razor, an Edwardian affair said to have belonged to the Duke of Windsor, a gift from the late Wallis Simpson, the American divorcee.

## The Secret Lives of London Detectives

Jessica's class was going to a petting zoo. Emily was taking the morning off to be one of the adults on the field trip. Squeezing past him in the hall, she put a camera in Judah's hand, saying, "Here."

Having removed her from her bath, Judah Zukor had his daughter Amy in his arms, swaddled in a towel. He could smell from her hair that he'd missed some shampoo, should have rinsed her head again. He had to look past his daughter's little rump to see what he'd been given. Her head was tucked in to the hollow of his shoulder. The child was going back to sleep. "Come on, Puppet, none of that. We've got to get moving. What's this?"

Emily answered, "What does it look like, Judah. A camera."

"What's wrong, doesn't it work?"

"I wouldn't know."

It was one of those foolproof numbers that wound its own film, focused itself. Still, where in the hell did you open the thing? Where did you put the batteries? "What do you mean you wouldn't know? It's your camera, Emily, not mine."

"I've forgotten *how* it works. I need to make sure *that* it works. Okay?" Emily had this way of letting him know she needed more from Judah than he was providing. You. You and your intermittent father act. She did this same thing in bed if he reached over to touch her. What I need from you Judah is help, not a roll in the clover. I've never been more stressed, Judah. I'm dying here, or haven't you noticed?

Judah was half-dressed and late to get started. Amy slumped over like a rag doll when he propped her up in her bed, the lower berth of a shaky wooden bunk. He got down on his knees and began foraging through her drawer of underthings. The carpet was cheap, more nylon than wool, and the nap burned his skin. Searching for her stuffed bunny beneath the piles of clothes and toys that were strewn about the floor, Jessica slid beneath him as if he were a bridge. "Help me get your sister dressed, Jess," he said.

"I'm looking for bunny," she protested.

"You can't take bunny to school anymore, remember? They won't let you. You're too big."

"Then I'm not going. I'm staying home. Help me look, Daddy."

"Where did you last see bunny, Puppet? Try to think. Did you have bunny with you while you were eating your breakfast?"

"I haven't had my breakfast yet. Amy didn't do her homework."

For no reason he could determine, Amy, waking now, began to whimper. He thought perhaps she had hit her head or otherwise injured herself but she hadn't. Increasingly, they had to look to Jessica to serve as an intermediary.

"Amy doesn't have homework."

"Amy does too have homework, Daddy. She brings a book home from class every day. She has to be read a story, then you have to sign a paper."

"When did this start?"

"It's in her knapsack, just see if it's not. She'll need money today for a tea as well."

A phone rang in the distance. Dishes piled high in the sink toppled over as Emily answered the call. She turned on the tap. He heard her speaking into the receiver as she answered, as well the chime of the microwave: something, waffles if the girls were lucky. He heard her open the microwave door, reset the timer, give the dish a little longer.

"You're going to need your shoes and stockings as well."

"NO. Not until I find bunny."

Jessica had dressed herself. He could see what she had done. She had put the dress on backwards so that the buttons up the back were in front, making it easier to work them. Two ends of an untied cinch now trailed the floor behind her. He heard Emily's footfalls returning toward their end of the house, heard her stop at the tub and release Amy's bathwater. Heard her put the rubber bottle of children's shampoo back where it belonged. She was carrying Amy's night dress in her hand when she came into the room. She had rinsed it out in the bathwater, apparently. She seemed to be wringing the neck of a Disney character that was stenciled on its front. "It's for you," said Emily. "The electrician."

"Tell him I'll call him back."

"He's been trying to get in here for weeks, Judah. You're never home when he rings. Take it up."

"I can't."

"Judah, the fuses pop over whenever I have more than two kitchen appliances working at the same time. Sometimes the outlets spark. It can't go on like that, it has to be dangerous. We've got to get him in here to look at it."

"Get him in then. I'm not stopping you."

"Who's going to be here, are you? I can't be here. And we can't just leave it unlocked. We don't have much, but what we do have is all right here in this house."

Judah straightened up to talk to Emily without realizing that Amy had crawled down from the bed and was trying to do what her sister had done, use him as a bridge. It was all he could do to keep his balance and stave off a fall that might have injured them both.

"Have what's-her-name let him in, the babysitter. Amy, stop it!"

"He can only come in the mornings, Judah. That's why he's calling here now. He's on his way. He's calling from his truck."

"What do you mean *he can only come in the morning?* What's that, some kind of rule made up by the electrician fairy? He's making a living, right?"

"I was lucky to get him."

"I can't be here this morning. I've got things I have to do."

"We have things we have to do as well, Judah. Myself and the girls. I'm not rescheduling this for you again. I told you this was going to happen. Are you going to talk to him or not?"

"I've got to get to work, Emily, I'm late as it is."

Emily bent over to pick something off the floor, the camera. He'd lost track of it somehow and it had been abandoned amidst all the other debris. "You stay here and deal with the electrician, Judah, or I'm not going to be here when you get home tonight. And neither will your daughters. Look at me. Do you understand? This time, I really won't be here."

He listened as she corralled their children toward the kitchen, saying, "Come on, girls, get dressed. We're late and you haven't had your breakfast yet."

\*

A large billboard advertising the London Zoo showed an ark being boarded in pairs beneath the caring eye of Noah. The last of the animals on the gangplank were cheery, lovesick tortoises with oversized oval eyes and puckering mouths that met in a kiss. Their rear legs and bobbing heads were operated by an electrical motor. Bassett was driving. He watched them from the intersection. Then he made a turn into traffic.

Bassett had once been handed a tortoise as a child. Assuming it was a stone, he'd asked if he could hold it, actually, then its thick, furious legs, beating the wind in any attempt to get away, had given him a start. He'd always been large for his age, thought stupid. This had happened in a classroom and cemented that impression. All the other children laughed. He was stupid, and now fearful as well.

His partner made of the sign something different. Judah thought, No wonder marriages fall apart so easily. Neither party understood what the other was looking for. Men assumed you paired off for company and sex. Women assumed you paired off to talk and to breed. They were similar enough, these impressions, to go by a common name, *falling in love*, close enough in conception to appear at a glance to be one and the same. They weren't, however, were they? Judah envisioned this as a joke on the whole human race. The Fates, he thought to himself, must have a dark sense of humor.

"You and Jane ever think about children, Bassett?"

"We talked about it, sure. But, you know, Zuk — children! How could we manage?"

"Right. I know. Jane never brings it up though? I thought she might. Most women would, sooner or later."

"It's never been an issue."

"No. I suppose not."

"Not with our work. You know what it's like. Times are uncertain. We don't see how you do it, you and Emily."

"Right. How's her job, she still with the estates agents, your Jane?"

"I talked to Jane, by the way. She said she'd set up a show-about when you and Emily were ready. Things any better between the two of you, Zuk?"

"Coming along — We had a row this morning, actually."

"Yeah, over what?"

"Electrician. Wanted me to wait till he got there this morning."

"And?"

"And I didn't."

"How was last Saturday night? You never said. Make your way through the minefield, did you?"

"The inlaws?"

"What's he hate about you most, that you're short, or that you're Jewish?"

"Chaplinesque."

Years ago, Judah's father-in-law had described him to a third party they knew in common as "Chaplinesque," meaning he was a Jew. With his mass of curly black hair and dark eyes that set in his spare face like saucers, he looked a bit like Charlie Chaplin, actually — which was to say, he supposed, like Chaplin he was compact of build, wiry in a way one associates with dancers and acrobats, and, like Chaplin, semitic. Put a bit of friction tape beneath his nose, a shabby bowler hat on his head and bamboo cane in his hand — yes, Chaplinesque, he supposed. No need for the oversized shoes or the splayed walk. Even in the absence of the rest of the costume, you could recognize the personage. At some masque ball, you'd know who he'd come as.

He heard about this through Emily, his bride, who thought it was funny. "Charlie Chaplin then?" Judah had asked. "Is that what he said, is it? I'm not sure how to take that."

Suppressing a smile, Emily had turned her back to him, trying to stave off a row. Anything having to do with her father could get Judah going. "Charlie Chaplin, that's all. Well, Chaplin — *with an attitude.*"

Emily had laughed, in this soft, sweet laugh she used to have, and the steam let out of his objection, Judah then laughed as well, saying, "Oh, right. Well, that makes it easier to hear, doesn't it." Of course, that had been when they still liked one another, a very long time ago.

Judah thought of what lay ahead of him, the evening to come. Despite her ultimatum, Emily would return to the house with the girls, electrician or no. Where else could she go to, her parents? Wouldn't that be a wheeze?! Maybe it was better the other way around. Spend a few days away himself, maybe longer. Give things a chance to cool down.

That was probably the smart thing. A few days apart wouldn't hurt either one. Who'd want to end up like so many others? Hamstringing the kids in a custody fight. Divorces fought out with bazookas. Yeah, a few days apart was the right thing to do, for things were coming to the point where they'd one day explode.

Judah opened the case file. "Which one's this again?"

"Lawrence. Gave his wife quite a beating. Good he came to his senses, might have beat her to death."

"Good she got to a phone."

Bassett asked, "What's Emily's dad building now, did he show you?"

"A galleon. He's up to the rigging, actually. Making it to scale. I helped him after dinner. I can still smell the glue on my fingers. He never knows what to do with them once he's finished, of course. Odd, that. I don't see the point. But he seems to enjoy it."

"Gives him something to do with his time, I imagine."

"That's what I've heard, Bassett. Can we do all this and still get you to the inquest in time to give your testimony?"

"Been postponed."

"Oh."

"Read me the address."

"It's up ahead. Lawrence, Florence Lawrence. She's still pressing charges?"

"While we're there, let's talk to the neighbor on the other side again, Mr. Bleakhouse."

"Then we'll go from door to door."

"Mr. Bleakhouse: He remind you a little of Thigpen, Zuk?"

"The Chesterfield cottage. Right."

The Chesterfields' cottage had been within walking distance of a Tudor school and a gray flint parish church, the picture of domesticity. It's odd, what you remember, Bassett thought. The teapot on the table, a midday paper spread out its full width, a pepper pot. Thigpen, of course. How dainty he'd been, how methodical. He'd fixed himself a bite to eat, read the paper, then washed the dishes in the sink and stacked them in the drainer. Surprised the couple on a lazy afternoon. The two of them trussed up like that. You could see it in their faces, something terrible had happened. They were sure they were dead.

Then Thigpen, the woman's first husband, reclining in an easy chair, a box of matches in his lap, a glass of ginger-pop on the floor beside him. His shoes were off. He'd made himself at home.

You could smell the gas from several blocks away. His partner had been the first through the door. The room was such that Thigpen was hidden. He was a thin, sorry little man with thin flaxen hair. People had probably been entering rooms without seeing him for most of Thigpen's life.

Thigpen said, "She never made it easy. I tried to get on. It's really not my fault. Life's full of funny things, ain't it. She's cold, that's all, she's not a warm person. But I love her all the same. You understand, I hope. I didn't come here intending no harm. I just couldn't go on without her. We're both of us Catholic, you see. We don't do with divorce. She's cast her mortal soul away. Now I'm casting mine. We'll be hand in hand in hell for all of eternity. I thought she'd go along, but you can see she was very resistant. I don't know what else to say, really. It's the only way I can think to keep us together. I must have passed the point where it was safe to let go."

A clock struck from the mantelpiece. Zuk dropped his weapon. Hands raised, he moved toward the man in the chair cooing words of assurance. As he moved, Thigpen brought up the box and a match. Bassett froze in the doorway. He was not, precisely, frightened, rather there was nothing about the situation that was real enough to respond to. He thought to himself, Any second now I will hear a siren and the police will arrive and they will know what to do.

"It was a legitimate shoot, Bassett."

"I never said it wasn't."

"He would have blown us all to kingdom come if you hadn't stepped in when you did. I told you so at the time."

The truth was that Bassett was shaken by the thought of the inquest, of recounting yet again what had happened. He'd told the story so many times to so many officials, it had begun to be like reconstructing a bad dream after waking in a sweat. And he'd yet to be asked about what bothered him most. He had come within a hair's breadth of failing to act. He'd had but a split second to decide if Thigpen was extending the matches for his partner Judah to take, or igniting an explosion, and Bassett had come as close as a man can to doing nothing at all. He simply couldn't believe he was facing the end of everything, not in some freshly swept cottage with a kettle on the burner. Perhaps if the setting had been different, if Thigpen had been wearing a ski mask or a stocking over his face.

Numbed, Bassett had been counting the strokes of the clock when he should have been acting on instinct. He might not be so lucky in the future. Ever since the incident, he had been dreaming at night of explosives. Fuses, blasting caps, *plastique*. Bombs that were ticking away at night in a closet. Things that went off in his hands when he touched them. Senseless deaths that he'd been helpless to prevent.

"Right, you did, you said it at the time, Zuk."

"So, forget it then. Put the Chesterfields behind you."

"You're the one who brought it up, Zuk, not me."

"Only because I know you as well as I do. You need to talk things out. Always have. For as long as we've been together."

"I told you, I'm okay."

"Do like I have. Put that sort of thing behind you. Take it day by day, from now on."

The truth was, Judah hadn't put the shooting behind himself at all. He remembered it clearly. They'd probably paid cash for their cottage, not borrowed from their in-laws, the way Judah had done. Pretty little place with a yard for kids to play their games in, bordered by hawthorn hedges. There'd been a bicycle near the front door with a rusty bell on its handlebars. Thigpen's.

Thigpen had showered, shaved, and splashed some of Chesterfield's pre-shave on his cheeks, so that when Judah opened the door there was a faint whiff of Yardley's beneath the overpowering stench of gas that filled the room. Thigpen worked as a milliner. He'd been dressed in black from head to toe. The round from Bassett's gun threw Thigpen over the back of the recliner in a flurry of black cloth and stocking feet and nothing left to hope for. There. Despite himself, he remembered it. And much more clearly than he cared to.

"Jencks," Bassett said. "*Mr. Bleakhouse.*"

"What?"

"The Lawrence woman's neighbor. The one you called Mr. Bleakhouse. Moved here from Scotland when his wife left him cold, remember? His name is Jencks. Said he used to be a milliner, or was that somebody else?"

"That's it, Franklin Jencks. The lonely little man, remember?"

"I remember."

\*

Jencks was still in his pajamas, working up a scrapbook. He'd been finishing his breakfast. He had a plate in his hand, a half-eaten crumpet with a dab of gluey apricot jam on the side of the plate. He'd probably been carrying it around the flat since he took it from the toaster that morning, nibbling it to death. His flesh was that whitish-silverish color of the critically ill and dying, and around his sunken cheeks there were whiskers he had missed. He wasn't a man who would have much of an appetite. He offered them tea.

"If you're sure it's no bother," Judah replied.

"So you remember us then?" asked Bassett.

"Oh yes, Mr. Bassett, I remember you perfectly, you and Inspector Zukor in addition. Please, gentlemen, sit down. I'll only be a minute, I'll have a cup as well, I think. I don't always keep a kettle on, you see. Not when you live by yourself. I might have a lemon to go with. I'll look."

"We wouldn't want to inconvenience you," said Judah.

"We won't be long," said Bassett.

"It doesn't matter. Here, let me take your coats. I was

only catching up on some unfinished business. It's the little things I never seem to be able to find time for."

He ran water. Pipes groaned. Bassett listened for the strike of a match. He heard coughing instead.

"It's decent of you to visit. Sit anywhere you'd like," Jencks called. "I don't know what I can do to help you. I'm afraid I told you all I know the last time you popped by. If I'd have thought of something else, I'd have saved you the bother of coming."

Judah looked for a place to sit down. A ray of light was coming through the window. The dust in the air was visible. "Are you sure we're not interrupting?" he asked.

Jencks soon returned. "Not at all, my day's free. This miserable cold," Jencks explained, coughing back phlegm, poking himself in the chest with his thumb. He waited for Bassett to explain why they'd come.

"We were wondering if you could tell us anything else."

"The night in question. Mr. Jencks."

"I don't know him well, like I told you. Like I told you, when I see him, I speak. He does in addition. The Lawrences keep to themselves. So do I. Pleasant, I can say. Quiet. Always considerate. That's how I'd describe them both. Others should as well. I don't mind going so far as to say that if you meant to find one person in the building to speak against either one of them, you'd have a job. Is she going to be all right? I saw her face as they were wheeling her out. It gave me quite a turn, I don't mind admitting. What an awful thing, what happened!" He shook his head at the memory. "Strange. Couples never see it coming, do they?" Jencks coughed.

"Sir?"

Judah looked around. Jencks' Kew Garden flat was furnished in the shabby genteel style of men who divorce after years of being married. There was a shortwave radio on the table. There was a broken grandfather clock beside it that had probably set on a mantelpiece when the family was together.

You knew you were seeing what he got in the settlement, Judah thought, a long dead overstuffed divan that sagged in the middle, a standing lamp with a tasseled shade, a threadbare oriental rug that seemed to be dying of thirst. All this Victoriana had more to do with a woman's taste than it ever had to do with his own, and you knew how it came to be there without needing to ask. At some point he'd probably thrown up his hands and said, Hell, I'm too tired to quarrel, it's only furniture, let's just get on with this — If it's really that important to you, then take what you want and leave what you don't!

"Well, I can't see how it would matter — There is one thing though."

"What's that, sir?"

"Well, they had a dog. Jigs, I think its name was. A longhaired thing, red dachshund? It got so it couldn't be apart from the wife. Don't ask me why. It would howl when she left in the morning and whine and scratch at the door. Someone complained, I suppose. I think they made her get rid of it, I think that's what he said. He thought the best thing to do was to have it put down. His idea, not hers, you see. We had a dog once, you see. I had to do the dirty work. Kidneys in our case. It was the right thing to do, but they blamed me just the same. God knows why, that's what happened though."

"What brings this to mind, Mr. Jencks, can you tell us?"

"Well Mr. Bassett, it was something he said. We talked about it once, Mr. Lawrence and me. He told me his story and I told him mine. Said it might have been harder, said it was small dog, not a big one, said it wasn't such a hard thing to do. Putting it down, he meant. I thought that was odd, don't you? It's just me, maybe, but I wouldn't think its size would matter, not when you were putting it down." He coughed. "But that isn't what you asked me, is it. What was it again you wanted to know?"

After Jencks, there were others to see.

\*

Bassett arrived home to find Jane asleep on their couch, still in her work clothes. Sitting across from her now at their kitchen table, Bassett thought Jane took longer to wake up from a nap than anyone he knew who enjoyed a beating pulse. It completely threw off her system. She awoke dazed, confused, disoriented, uncertain of what day it was, unsure of where she was, then took hours to re-cover. It was hard to describe, this look of hers. It was a look he'd seen on the face of cadavers. Young women, that is. Not men. It put him in mind of an adolescent who'd been sent off to camp on holiday, only to find no one her age when she finally arrived.

Holding a mug of coffee between two hands as if holding it for warmth, Jane said, "I'm going to the grocers."

"This evening?"

"What should I get?"

Bassett listed several things he knew they were low on. Staples, primarily.

She made no move to rise, get a pad, make a list. Just to see what she would do, he railed off several things he knew you couldn't get from their green grocer, calipers, a micrometer gauge, thirty-gauge chrome-nickel wire. "Get In-home if they've got it, don't try to pinch pennies by buying some generic."

Jane looked into the coffee she was holding as if it contained something she'd forgotten she wanted. "Anything else? You ate the red and yellow peppers both, then left over the bells. No more bell peppers, I assume. No more broccoli neither. It just went to waste."

"Well, if you find them on sale, I could use a few lengths of one-centimeter copper tubing, I imagine. Make each of them, oh, I don't know, say six centimeters long. If you have to take longer than that, I can always cut them down here at home. Once I have the wire, all I have left to acquire is a six volt battery and a switch. You got the fulminate powder I asked for last time, didn't you?"

"If you asked for it, Bassett, I got it."

"Right. I thought you probably did."

She sipped her drink. The coffee, apparently, was cold. She put down her cup. With the tip of one finger, Jane traced the petals of the indeterminate flowers in the pattern of the table cloth. "Is that it?"

"That should do it. It's almost complete, you see."

"What? What's almost complete?"

"Well, there's still the plutonium. I'll have to get the plutonium — don't ask me from where, Jane. I'm not at liberty to say."

"What?"

"I've only gotten as far as the detonator, you see. Fortunately your mother got me the firing circuit for Christmas last year, bless her heart. That sped things up a bit, didn't it. Did I tell you I wrote her and offered her thanks?"

"Who? Wrote who, my mother? You hate my mother, always have. You can't stand to be in the same room with her, either one of you. You wrote to my mother?"

"Not a long letter, just a note. She's helped me in other ways as well, did I tell you? It was the dear old girl herself who said, Basset me boy? Let me tell you, fuse wire melts when you get it too hot. You can't just use any wire at all, it's got to be special."

"Special?"

"Oh, yes indeed, Jane my dear. You don't think I came up with chrome-nickel wire on my own, do you? Give credit where credit is due. How else but through your mum would I know what to ask for? Now, I'm sort of a tin-cap-insulator wire-packing-material sod myself. But your mother, Jane? Your mother's much more sophisticated when it comes to explosives. Oh yes. Did you know she served as an advisor to a key Al Quaeda cell?"

"Sophisticated? My mother? What are you talking about?"

"The design, Jane."

The phone rang in the other room. "That's probably her right now. We're in this together, did I tell you?"

"Tell me what?"

"Oh yes, I'm not going this alone."

"Should I get it? It's probably Judah. How much longer are the two of you going to be in Domestic Disputes?"

Bassett answered, "No, let it ring."

"All right, I'll get it then, if that's what you want."

She returned shortly thereafter. She took the chair across from his, retrieved her cup, sipped from the cup, stared down into the coffee. "It's for you."

"Who is it?"

"Mum. She said to tell you that copper tubing wasn't worth piss unless you sealed the firing leads with wax at each end."

"Who is it really?"

Jane looked up. "Judah. Who do you think?"

\*

Judah arrived home by sunset. Emily was there, and so were the girls. She had the *Shabbat* candles on the table in the kitchen. Beside them was the heel of a loaf of bread and a paper cup of juice rather than the requisite glass of wine.

On the table as well was the rest of the loaf, a sheath of her papers from work, a butane lighter and a three-tiered candle in the shape of a snowman that the girls liked to use as a *shamus*, a CD of children's songs that was caked in spots with jam and chocolate, assorted plastic beads meant to look like wild animals, a one-inch heel from a navy blue pump, a workbook page of upper and lower case letters, a plastic cornice from a Barbie playhouse that might have been made from pink sugar, the receiver of a cordless phone, a Rolodex so overcome with entries that now it was blossoming business cards (two of these new electricians), a children's book on basic nutrition that had a haricot vert on its cover, a flea collar missing its buckle that one of the girls had discovered outside, a pack of circuit breakers, an atomizer and lip gloss, a half-eaten apricot and three brittle fig rolls, a Glengarry hat made of construction paper that had straight sides that were coming unglued and a crease along the top and three lengths of fuzzy colored yarn in the back.

Judah walked into his house through the kitchen door just as one of Emily's mates from work was departing through the living room. His wife and the fellow were laughing now. He'd meant to sneak in through the back door and surprise the girls with his presence — perhaps this was more of a surprise than he'd meant. The young man said, "You don't know what it means to me. You've saved my life."

Emily answered, "Don't be silly. Keep it for as long as you want it."

"You're always there, you know? You're always there when I can't manage on my own."

"That's because I'm a central figure in your life right now. I've got responsibilities, don't I."

"Right. But you could be a central figure in my life and still not know what I need."

"What, be a husband, you mean?"

He couldn't make out what she said next, for she lowered her voice. Then he heard her close their front door, and walk to the bathroom. Judah unearthed the telephone receiver from the mound of domestic debris and placed a phone call to Bassett. Jane came on the line, then went to get her husband.

"What is it, Zuk, what's up?"

"We've put it behind us. I'm home, the girls are fine, she's home. Everything's back to normal."

"Just one of those passing storm clouds then."

"I thought you might be worried."

"Well, you know — Where kids are involved — How was the zoo, did they say?"

"Had the time of their lives."

"Great."

"Right."

"Fine, Zuk."

"It's different once there's kids."

"That's what you've always said."

"It's bumpier. That's all I'm saying."

"Well, look — Jane and I are off to shopping."

Judah said, "You watch where you step, you test every tread. It's manageable."

"Zuk, so long as it's settled, right, that's the main thing."

"Right. Well, great. I'll let you go then."

Emily came upon Judah in their kitchen as if she'd been expecting a prowler. She said, "You scared me. I heard you stirring about out here and thought someone had broken in. You just missed Cecil. Darn. I do wish you could have met him. What are you doing here, by the way?" Waiting to be kissed, she took him by his elbows.

Kissing her lightly on the cheek, he said, "I live here, remember? Where are the girls?"

"I gave them away."

"Any mail?"

"Haven't looked yet. How was your day?"

"Couldn't have been better. How was yours, any problems?"

"I watched a little of 'Mary Poppins' with the girls while getting them into their play clothes."

"That was the highpoint, not the zoo?"

"I would have preferred 'Born Free', actually. 'Mary

Poppins' was the girls' selection."

"A story with more depth then?"

"Something with animals."

"How's your new charge, Emily?"

"Cecil? He's young. I think he'll work out though. Training someone just doubles your caseload. He's buying a house, did I tell you? In Marivole."

"On an intern's pay? He doesn't know what he's letting himself in for, does he?"

"He wants me to help him furnish it."

"Like you could spare the time."

Emily opened a kitchen cabinet. She was in her stocking feet, standing on tiptoes. Moving tinned food around, she said, "We'll be getting supper on, if that's what you've come for. Help me clear the table, can you?"

"I'll start pasta for the girls. Should we light the candles now? It's nearly dark."

Emily misunderstood. "Electricity's on, in here at least. That's his bid for rewiring, up there on the fridge."

"Did you get us out of tomorrow night?"

"It slipped my mind. Completely forgot. Sorry."

"There's no way to leave me at home, I suppose. It's the girls they want to see, not me."

"The girls are their grandchildren, Judah. They've got a right to see their grandchildren."

"What about me, don't I have rights as well?"

"We won't stay long. Just don't start a row with Dad, that only makes it worse for everyone."

"I'm not the one who starts them, am I? We couldn't put this off until Sunday, I suppose."

"Whatever, Judah. This one time though, if not for me

for the girls, try to find a common ground with him. That's all I'm asking."

The phone rang. Emily took it. The kitchen was so small that she had to squeeze between Judah and the table to reach it. Removing an earring, she smiled at him uncomfortably, trying to make the best of things.

As she passed, he thought she smelled of her day. She smelled faintly of urine as well.

Judah went looking for his daughters, calling out, "I hear children, I hate children, when I find children in my house I can't help but tickle them!" Screams of mock fright were heard to come from their room.

# The Falconer

At the age of twenty-seven, Morris came to work for Lord and Lady Adderley as a falconer and when the lord of the manor died and his wife closed the rookery, she provided for Morris by allowing him to stay on in the small but comfortable quarters above the multiple car garages, this in return for becoming her chauffeur, believing as she did that a display of charitable conduct to the lowborn was required of their betters once there'd been a suitable display over time of their loyalty. Morris mastered early-on how to make himself a fixture in her particular station of life. Lady Adderley would have thought nothing of undressing before him or disclosing her dearest secrets to a lover while Morris stood at her shoulder, for, on duty, he had no more human presence than does an expensive potted fern beneath an elaborate *porte-cochère*. Morris, in other words, had mastered the art of servitude and become during twenty years as her chauffeur what might appear to outsiders to be a nondescript, middle aged man, but to those who appreciate the intricacies of what remains of British manor life, he had become, instead, one of the staff.

The ready-furnished quarters in which Morris lived were part of a highly prized mews on the Adderley estate, that is, an area that included stables and carriage houses as well as conversions done in the 1920s for garages and autos, all built around a cobblestone courtyard. She was housebound by this point — Lady Adderley, that is — an invalid, and with no one to motor about any longer and all but one of her cars sold off, this a four-door Buick Regal, Morris had learned to fill his days with a list of small and still smaller domestic tasks, such as scrubbing the floors or repapering a guest room. Round-the-clock nurses had become impossible to keep and he was counting out her dosages of medicine for the week ahead, organizing a myriad of pills and capsules into intersecting lines so that they mirrored the pattern of the cobblestone below, when he learned that he was to take the car to London and fetch a new girl from Marylebone Station who had, for whatever reason, agreed to make her home here.

When he opened the passenger door she went around to the other side and sat in the back, and after that they exchanged but a very few words until an accident between a lorry and an ancient Triumph Spitfire forced them off the M at Leamington Spa. Morris was negotiating the narrow lanes of Warwick and Coventry which, through some inexplicable phenomenon of mass self-deception, are locally regarded as thoroughfares.

"How do you come to be doing the meds, Morris?" the girl asked.

He explained. With an unaccustomed candor, he discussed how he'd come to the Adderley estate to begin with, describing the lord as a high old bird of colorful plumage and his wife as a decent sort who rewarded her most trusted and trustworthy staff less in her time on earth than later, believing they should go to a better reward at the same time she did hers, albeit hers of a different sort.

"So she has you in her will, does she?"

He answered, "You're new then? From London? Did you nurse as well in London?"

"I couldn't find work. I worked in a scent shop. What's out there in those fields?"

"What?"

"You know. Out there. Rabbits?"

"Sometimes there's rabbits. Why?"

"I've never seen a rabbit in a field, that's all."

"You will, now that you live in the country. You'll see them all the time."

"Will I? White whiskered rabbits, like in nursery rhyme books? Mostly what I've found in fields in the country so far is rubbish, not rabbits."

"It's because of the tourists. They leave it behind. They're a piggy bunch, tourists. The Germans are worst."

"Are you married, Morris?"

"No. Never been."

"But you have your own place."

"Yes, I have my own quarters, you will as well."

"So you have your peace and quiet. All by yourself. Out here in the sticks. What's she like, the old girl, tell me some more, rich as all sin?"

"Lady Adderley?"

"We could kill her, you and me, and divide all the money."

Morris's eyes caught her own in the mirror. He was shocked to discover that he felt a pleasurable flutter of excitement at such a ridiculously inappropriate remark.

"Relax. It was just a joke. You look like a rabbit that's been caught in two headlamps. You should see your face, imagine!"

He said, "You're not the sort I'd picture working as a live-in. What brings you out to us?"

"I'm no angel and it seems a cozy place to work. Besides, it isn't forever."

Morris said, "It's not always easy to find another situation. A job's a job, right? Clientele mostly women, where you worked in your scent shop?"

"Mostly men, actually, buying presents for their wives. Confidentially, there was lechers right and left. Most of them hovered over you, trying to see what they could get, you know."

"Well you won't have that with us."

"I could do with a few more girls my own age, I suppose. Leaves me no one to talk to."

"You could always talk to me. What was it like, selling scent?"

"I mean, just give it a thought. A snotty scent shop, right? It's *so* not me." She leaned forward in the backseat so that her arms and head were up in front with Morris. "Say, who are you, anyway? What's any of this to you, huh?"

"I'm the police."

This seemed to amuse her. She said, "I thought you were somebody else."

\*

Nora, her name was Nora, wasn't pretty exactly. She had large brown eyes beneath a pail broad forehead that seemed out of proportion to such a thin, anemic face. But she possessed that shining vitality of the young and unfettered, and he felt sufficiently starved for vitality to begin observing the girl from afar as she struck up flirty little relationships with two of the gardeners and several of the delivery men.

Since he'd never really entered into commerce with women when he himself had been young, Morris did not understand the shrewd intelligence with which someone Nora's age can be on a guard against a man to whom she thinks she's revealed more than she meant to. Nora spent her days waiting on Lady Adderley hand, finger, and foot, not oblivious to Morris at all. She knew his every step. They negotiated the estate at a safe but wary distance from one another, much as the two proverbial ships are said to pass in the night, and the whole business might have been plain sailing had things been otherwise than they obviously were.

Weeks could go by during which they would not exchange more than two or three words in the course of a day and then at some unexpected and often inopportune moment she might confide to him with an air of unbridled intimacy a hairline fracture in her quite obviously broken heart. Shamelessly, he was a comfort. He was fascinated.

In Morris's world there was a place for everyone and everything, hence everyone to their place, while in hers, well, Nora *was* her world. So fully did she occupy each inch of its earth and take its air into her lungs! So near as he could tell, she was incapable of pity of others, indifferent to any suffering but her own, contemptuous of all good intentions that did not in some way bring about immediate personal benefit to her and her alone. While the rest of us toast ourselves over the fires of human companionship, she was cold to the bone. She was petty, ruthless, and scheming. She was predatory. At the thought of any injustice real or perceived, her pupils opened and hardened, and while this was no doubt impossible, he had the impression that her neck stiffened as well so that, like that of a fowl of prey, her head seemed to turn on its stem as if held in place by a bolt and a screw.

To have her in his presence was to be no less alone than when he was completely without her; she lived apart from him or anyone else, untouched. She said ridiculous things, in ridiculous ways, "Get your butt out of tinsel town" or "Totally have to;" yet he looked forward to having her with him with a growing and sometimes insatiable hunger. Never before had Morris encountered any human being like her. In a world of the inchoate, he was partial, Nora was whole.

She was also felonious. She concocted farfetched schemes to get the better of Lady Adderley, all with Morris as her accomplice, some of them frivolous and comic, but others so thoroughly thought out she had them down to the detail. None of these he embraced, of course, but once Nora was out of his sight he found himself troubled and moved. It was as if Nora had meant to turn his attention to erosions in the mortar of a wall, when all Morris had been able to perceive was the pattern of the brick. Working for the rich and the very rich particularly is to be daily reminded of how unevenly the pleasures of life are distributed and how much is an accident of birth. Grooming a falcon does not teach one to fly, after all; rather it reminds us we are bipeds. And something similar might be said about observing the young and the casually in love when one is middle-aged, living by one's self, a chauffeur driving an American Buick.

For the first time in his life, Morris swaddled the suspicion that he'd been brought this close to great sums of money through an intricate and well-wrought design. He knew there were cheques about the house that arrived each week in the post. A cheque could be washed — or so he understood — so that a draft made out in one name could be made to appear to be meant for someone else. He fantasized an intricate scheme whereby he established a new identity altogether, several identities, actually, respectable identities, a businessman, an architect, moving from village to village, from bank to bank, but the scheme was always more clear in his mind than the intricacies themselves. Morris had a forger's desires — not one's polish. He simply was who he was. He could not quite shake the newly found feeling that he'd been meant to be a rich man, one of those men whose ship has come in, yet he could get no closer to it than this scheme, for every time he tried to imagine himself appearing before the cage of a teller dressed to the nines, his hands and wrists seemed to dangle out of the jacket he was wearing. He wasn't cut out for thieving. No matter how long he tried to make his trousers, they were never quite long enough.

"Nora," said Morris, "enough now, this is madness you realize. It's completely, totally mad. I don't want any part of it. *Any* of it."

"No?"

"It's wrong, all of these schemes of yours, they're wrong simply wrong. I don't know what could have been going through my mind. Or yours."

Morris, it seems, had that peculiarly English belief that generally passes for honesty or a respect for the law, namely, that while it is humiliating to beg on the street, it is more humiliating still to steal. He was casually fascinated — aren't we all? — by people of doubtful occupations and shifty purposes, but crimes of this magnitude were to him what a naughty snapshot might be to a boy who abuses himself in bed each night in private beneath a tent he makes of knees and sheets, strange, exciting. Good enough for a toss-off.

"I know," said Nora. "I know."

"I can't go through with any of this. I hope you see that."

"Oh Morris, it was only a game — I thought you knew that."

"Well game or not I'm finished with it."

"That's it then Morris? That's that?"

"That, my girl, is definitely that. I'll hear not another word. Now Lady Adderley is calling you and she'll expect you straight away."

\*

Yes, the whole business might have been plain sailing had Nora not appeared at his door that night unexpectedly with tears in her eyes.

"Can I come in?"

He'd put himself to bed at a reasonable hour and, awakened from his sleep as he was, Morris's hair shot up from the middle of his head like a geyser. After cinching his robe and plastering this ridiculous spout of hair to his skull with the flat of his hand, he answered, "What is it, Nora? Of course. Yes of course you may. Here. Come in."

"I've done an awful thing." She said this as she passed him, then collapsed in a chair and buried her face in her hands. Her shoulders quivered. He offered her a handkerchief.

She blew her nose with a honk. "Oh Morris," she

sighed, "it's clear I haven't had one drop of common sense until now, have I? We were almost caught. Don't you see?!" For a moment Morris assumed she meant these schemes of hers had somehow been exposed to Lady Adderley, or at least to some of her staff, but Nora told another tale instead.

She told a confused tale of meeting one of the gardeners in the tool shed. The point of this tale was that she'd been badly used in some way or other, of being two-timed or jilted or simply seduced then abandoned, but it was impossible to say for sure, just as it was impossible to say which of the two gardeners she'd met, and, having nothing of use to say in return, Morris cooed at her as long ago he'd cooed at his peregrine falcons. Surprisingly, it worked. He began to put a kettle on for tea as though they might be speaking for the rest of the night, but she curled into his arm like a child and they fell asleep instead.

"I think I may have lost my house key, on top of everything else. I must have dropped it in the tool shed."

"Where's this tool shed, Nora?" asked Morris.

She described it. "Oh that, said Morris. "That's the old rookery."

Thus began the next phase of their relationship. Nora would appear unexpectedly at his door in the middle of the night and ask Morris if he might let her in. She was too frightened now she explained to spend the night by herself.

He would awake next morning before dawn in his pitch-black room to find that Nora was gone. Apparently she'd let herself out at some point in the night, and while he came to expect this, there were moments when, just an instant, just when he was opening his eyes for the first time of the day, he thought he saw her there perched on the arm of his easy chair, perfectly balanced and completely at-one with the moment, but hungry most of all, ravenously, insatiably hungry.

At what point he began feeding her with his fingers is very hard to say. They began slipping away in the afternoons to take walks in the nearby fields and it was no doubt during one of these leisurely outings that he tucked a bit of lean beefsteak he'd nicked from the kitchen into her mouth, then — as if this were the most natural of things to do — covered her eyes with his hand while she swallowed.

In any case it was during one of these walks that she first took flight. They had reached the point where Nora starved herself, refused to take meals, refused anything and all, and if for some reason he had not remembered to secure meat from the cook, she would fly a few feet ahead of him, often in dangerous, arching patterns. He would let her pass by him upon her return, perhaps producing a bit of beefsteak after all, or mutton or hare or fowl, it didn't really matter so long as it came from his fingers, this time on a lure, always careful to put it out so that she might readily seize it and feed.

It was while he was snatching the lure away one day that her talons broke his skin and that night Morris dug to the bottom of his closet and found in a long forgotten trunk the thick leather gauntlet for his left hand. Within the month he'd found a ferrier nearby who cut from a set of old bridles the leather for the jesses and rufter hood, braided the leash, cannibalized from an old farm implement a very usable swivel, even found a bell. Perhaps no man has ever known a sweeter or more romantic moment with another person as Morris experienced fitting the first of the jesses they'd made to her ankle, or slipping the hood over her head while her eyes remained open; he closed them, making this sweeter still. There is a point, you see, where Heaven and Hell touch the soles of their shoes, where the darkness is light, where unbridled appetite seems demanding of all human rein, and this, for Morris, was very much that point. It was the cruelty of it, the fitting of that hood, how the braces could be drawn to keep her head from jerking. He found himself listening to a sound of his own making, a peculiar mix of click and whistle that he was making with his lips and his tongue, a sound he'd learned to make long ago.

\*

It was Nora, not Morris, who brought up the rookery first. She was becoming restless with her normal duties in the house, restless in the house itself, and frustrated with the padded pole he'd had built for his room where she slept now each night, fully hooded, fully fettered. When he least expected her to she might perch herself on the roof of a shed or take to the branches of a nearby tree when he snatched away a bit of meat by jerking on his lure. It was Nora who demanded that he train her. She preferred the leash to being left at hack. She longed for the hood; the crueler the fit, the better, Morris thought. It was as if she wanted to be tamed and broken the more blood-thirsty she became, the quicker he moved her along to larger and wilder game in the open. First he would hood her. Next he would remove the hood and rub the prey across her feet, inducing her to feed, brushing it across her legs, teasing her mouth. Then, as she picked at the flesh, Morris removed the hood, replaced it as she fed, removed it again.

Dorothy Parker once remarked that the difference between a pervert and the rest of us is that a pervert does the one thing in bed we won't — such are the games lovers play. This might have remained such a harmless lover's game had it not come to a head one drizzly, dank afternoon. As Nora was counting out the medicines she overheard two of Lady Adderley's solicitors discussing the old lady's will. For the past six months, since her latest stroke, solicitors from London had been arriving then leaving on a regular basis, but these two were new. They spoke about Lady Adderley as if they knew her only by description, yet they seemed perfectly decided in their opinion of who they would find, a difficult, demanding, and generally insufferable creature, who, as near as Nora could surmise, had gotten it into her head to leave everything to a charity, right down to her buttons. Nora took this directly to Morris.

Morris was pissed. Understandably. Nevertheless, it was at Nora's suggestion, not his, that they went into Bath on their first day free in common to see a solicitor of her acquaintance, someone named Dymer. Dymer, this white whiskered rabbit of a human being from the shadows of her past, told them Morris hardly dared hope to get so much as a penny, what a pity, the devil was always in the details, wasn't it; pity the honest man. It was all the old business from this chauffeur's point of view unless they seized the very moment and did all that they could to make ample amends that put him in line for what was hers, in whole or in part, which was to say, and in this sense, potentially, *his* in addition.

"What sort of *ample amends*?" asked Nora.

He told the couple about a little used provision of the law meant for those who realize they are losing their marbles, a Prohibitum of Perepeteia, that is, Prohibition against Reversal, which, Dymer explained, came first into being with mad King George. Superseding any will and testament drawn before it, it superseded as well all that might come after.

Nora was intrigued. "All we need is her signature?"

"All you need is her signature."

"How are we suppose to get it?" Morris asked.

"That's your affair, not mine."

Nora turned to Morris, but it was to Dymer she was speaking."She's not herself since she's had her last stroke."

"I'll leave it undated," said Dymer. "An oversight."

Clearly Morris wasn't convinced. "Who'd be fool enough to grant it, without having her present?

"I'll take care of that," Dymer replied.

"Who'd be fool enough to believe it?" asked Morris.

"You've been with her twenty years, you say? It's not out of the question."

"Her children won't sit still for this."

"Let them," said Dymer. "They'll make their case, we'll make ours, Nora."

"How long would this take?" she asked.

"Not more than a fortnight."

Said Nora, "We'll come back in a fortnight."

They caught a bus at the train station upon their return. The bus let him off at a crossroads and the pair returned to Lady Adderley's estate following the sandy footpath along the ever-familiar roadside, facing south toward the horizon where mowers were at work in a field on the edge of the estate. On a hill in the distance, two women in skirts who were more concerned with cruelty to animals than they were with how human beings could be cruel to one another were watching the workers through field glasses. The grass was high nearest the roadside, and alive with hundreds of new-born rabbits, some trusting enough to get near them. Set-tling into committing a crime you never thought yourself capable of is one of the few truly freeing moments in a per-son's life, and Morris returned to the estate as fresh as if he'd slept, enjoying the beautiful day with its thick clouds and a grayish sky with the sun breaking through.

"It's time we re-opened the rookery," said Nora.

"Now?"

"Yes, Morris. Now. It's my season." She explained what she wanted. A basket — perhaps a hamper — filled with straw. "Let's go there. It's time we went to the down."

Over the past few months he had been training her with herons and rooks at the down, the darkest and remotest area of Lady Adderley's estate. The first she'd take from his hand, the second he would kill by wringing its neck then toss into the distance, and the third he'd release on its own, letting her have it as her prey as he spun out her leash on its spool. Never had he dared to release her on her own. He knew there'd be no going back after that.

For the first time since the training began, he removed the leash and she soared, a flight of beauty, with all its predatory grace, their fates how tethered as one. All that was left was the rookery.

It is said, you'll recall, that no falconer can stare into the eyes of his bird since all the desires of a falcon are the color of flesh. One recoils or goes mad. Perhaps there is something to this, for as Morris awaited Nora's return, he opened the rookery for the first time in twenty years. Spider webs hung from the roof not in cylindrical designs but rather in sagging sheets, like ragged, yellowish linen. It was so disgusting to the touch that he found himself wiping it free from his face. After this he began on the clutter. The rookery had become a center of gravity for anything on the estate no longer in use but too good to throw away, and it was only after he had found a new home for the likes of broken milking stools and tilling implements that he learned its timber had been sorely used by dry rot. Virtually empty now, much about the rookery was so loose it looked as if it would come apart when given a tug, and the wiring had been so ill effected by the foul damp that each lamp would have to be done anew. After hammering nails until his hands rung, he set about mending the wire. He stuffed the cracks between the boards with newspaper and cleaned the floor as best he could, reminding himself of a pattern on his mattress that he used to be aware of while counting out meds. It was primrose, he thought.

Fomite
Burlington, Vermont

Fomite is a literary press whose authors and artists explore the human condition -- political, cultural, personal and historical -- in poetry and prose.

*A fomite is a medium capable of transmitting infectious organisms from one individual to another.*

"The activity of art is based on the capacity of people to be infected by the feelings of others." Tolstoy, *What is Art?*

**Flight and Other Stories** - J. Boyer

In *Flight and Other Stories,* we're with the fattest woman on earth as she draws her last breaths and her soul ascends toward its final reward. We meet a divorcee who can fly for no more effort than flapping her arms. We follow a middle-aged butler whose love affair with a young woman leads him first to the mysteries of bondage, and then to the pleasures of malice. Story by story, we set foot into worlds so strange as to seem all but surreal, yet everything feels familiar, each moment rings true. And that's when we recognize we're in the hands of one of America's truly original talents.

**AlphaBetaBestiario** - Antonello Borra

Animals have always understood that mankind is not fully at home in the world. Bestiaries, hoping to teach, send out warnings. This one, of course, aims at doing the same.

**Improvisational Arguments** - Anna Faktorovich

*Improvisational Arguments* is written in free verse to capture the essence of modern problems and triumphs. The poems clearly relate short, frequently humorous and occasionally tragic, stories about travels to exotic and unusual places, fantastic realms, abnormal jobs, artistic innovations, political objections, and misadventures with love.

Fomite
Burlington, Vermont

**Loisaida**  -  Dan Chodorokoff

Catherine, a young anarchist estranged from her parents and squatting in an abandoned building on New York's Lower East Side is fighting with her boyfriend and con-flicted about her work on an underground newspaper. After learning of a developer's plans to demolish a community garden, Catherine builds an alliance with a group of Puerto Rican community activists. Together they confront the confluence of politics, money, and real estate that rule Manhattan. All the while she learns important lessons from her great-grandmother's life in the Yiddish anarchist movement that flourished on the Lower East Side at the turn of the century. In this coming of age story, fam-ily saga, and tale of urban politics, Dan Chodorkoff explores the "principle of hope", and examines how memory and imagination inform social change.

**Still Time  -**  Michael Cocchiarale

*Still Time* is a collection of twenty-five short and shorter stories exploring tensions that arise in a vari-ety of contemporary relationships: a young boy must deal with the wrath of his out-of-work father; a woman runs into a man twenty years after an awk-ward sexual encounter; a wife, unable to conceive, imagines her own murder, as well as the reaction of her emotionally distant husband; a soon-to-be ten-ured English professor tries to come to terms with her husband's shocking return to the religion of his youth; an assembly line worker, married for thirty years, dis-covers the surprising secret life of his recently hospitalized wife. Whether a few hundred or a few thousand words, these and other stories in the col-lection depict characters at moments of deep crisis. Some feel powerless, overwhelmed—unable to do much to change the course of their lives. Others rise to the occasion and, for better or for worse, say or do the thing that might transform them for good. Even in stories with the most troubling of endings, there remains the possibility of redemption. For each of the characters, there is still time.

Fomite
Burlington, Vermont

**The Listener Aspires to the Condition of Music** - Barry Goldensohn

*"I know of no other selected poems that selects on one theme, but this one does, charting Goldensohn's career-long attraction to music's performance, consolations and its august, thrilling, scary and clownish charms. Does all art aspire to the condition of music as Pater claimed, exhaling in a swoon toward that one class act? Goldensohn is more aware than the late 19th century of the overtones of such breathing: his poems thoroughly round out those overtones in a poet's lifetime of listening."*

John Peck, poet, editor, Fellow of the American Academy of Rome

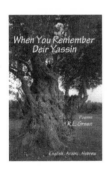

**When You Remember Deir Yassin** - R.L Green

*When You Remember Deir Yassin* is a collection of poems by R. L. Green, an American Jewish writer, on the subject of the occupation and destruction of Palestine. Green comments: "Outspoken Jewish critics of Israeli crimes against humanity have, strangely, been called "anti-Semitic" as well as the hilariously illogical epithet "self-hating Jews." As a Jewish critic of the Israeli government, I have come to accept these accusations as a stamp of approval and a badge of honor, signifying my own fealty to a central element of Jewish identity and ethics: one must be a lover of truth and a friend to the oppressed, and stand with the victims of tyranny, not with the tyrants, despite tribal loyalty or self-advancement. These poems were written as expressions of outrage, and of grief, and to encourage my sisters and brothers of every cultural or national grouping to speak out against injustice, to try to save Palestine, and in so doing, to reclaim for myself my own place as part of the Jewish people." The poems are offered in the original English with Arabic and Hebrew translations accompanying each poem.

Fomite
Burlington, Vermont

### The Co-Conspirator's Tale  -  Ron Jacobs

There's a place where love and mistrust are never at peace; where duplicity and deceit are the universal currency. *The Co-Conspirator's Tale* takes place within this nebulous firmament. There are crimes committed by the police in the name of the law. Excess in the name of revolution. The combination leaves death in its wake and the survivors struggling to find justice in a San Francisco Bay Area noir by the author of the underground classic *The Way the Wind Blew:A History of the Weather Underground* and the novel *Short Order Frame Up*.

### Roadworthy Creature, Roadworthy Craft  -  Kate Magill

Words fail but the voice struggles on. The culmination of a decade's worth of performance poetry, *Roadworthy Creature, Roadworthy Craft* is Kate Magill's first full-length publication. In lines that are sinewy yet delicate, Magill's poems explore the terrain where idea and action meet, where bodies and words commingle to form a strange new flesh, a breathing text, an "I" that spirals outward from itself.

### Carts and Other Stories - Zdravka Evtimova

Roots and wings are the key words that best describe the short story collection, *Carts and Other Stories*, by Zdravka Evtimova. The book is emotionally multilayered and memorable because of its internal power, vitality and ability to touch both the heart and your mind. Within its pages, the reader discovers new perspectives true wealth, and learns to see the world with different eyes. The collection lives on the borders of different cultures. *Carts and Other Stories* will take the reader to wild and powerful Bulgarian mountains, to silver rains in Brussels, to German quiet winter streets and to wind bitten crags in Afghanistan. This book lives for those seeking to discover the beauty of the world around them, and will have them appreciating what they have— and perhaps what they have lost as well.

Fomite
Burlington, Vermont

**Views Cost Extra** - L.E. Smith

Views that inspire, that calm, or that terrify – all come at some cost to the viewer. In *Views Cost Extra* you will find a New Jersey high school preppy who wants to inhabit the "perfect" cowboy movie, a rural mailman disgusted with the residents of his town who wants to live with the penguins, an ailing screen writer who strikes a deal with Johnny Cash to reverse an old man's failures, an old man who ponders a young man's suicide attempt, a one-armed blind blues singer who wants to reunite with the car that took her arm on the assembly line -- and more. These stories suggest that we must pay something to live even ordinary lives.

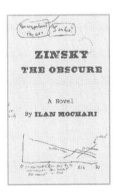

**Zinsky the Obscure** - Ilan Mochari

"If your childhood is brutal, your adulthood becomes a daily attempt to recover: a quest for ecstasy and stability in recompense for their early absence." So states the 30-year-old Ariel Zinsky, whose bachelor-like lifestyle belies the torturous youth he is still coming to grips with. As a boy, he struggles with the beatings themselves; as a grownup, he struggles with the world's indifference to them. *Zinsky the Obscure* is his life story, a humorous chronicle of his search for a redemptive ecstasy through sex, an entrepreneurial sports obsession, and finally, the cathartic exercise of writing it all down. Fervently recounting both the comic delights and the frightening horrors of a life in which he feels – always – that he is not like all the rest, Zinsky survives the worst and relishes the best with idiosyncratic style, as his heartbreak turns into self-awareness and his suicidal ideation into self-regard. A vivid evocation of the all-consuming nature of lust and ambition – and the forces that drive them – *Zinsky the Obscure* is a novel of extraordinary zeal, range, and power.

Fomite
Burlington, Vermont

### The Derivation of Cowboys & Indians - Joseph D. Reich

*The Derivation of Cowboys & Indians* represents a profound journey, a breakdown of The American Dream from a social, cultural, historical, and spiritual point of view. Reich examines in concise!detail the loss of the collective unconscious, commenting on our! contemporary postmodern culture with its self-interested excesses, on where and how things all go wrong, and how social/political practice rarely meets its original proclamations and promises. Reich's surreal and self-effacing satire brings this troubling message home. *The Derivations of Cowboys & Indians* is a desperate search and struggle for America's literal, symbolic, and spiritual home.

### Kasper Planet: Comix and Tragix - Peter Schumann

The British call him Punch, the Italians, Pulchinello, the Russians, Petruchka, the Native Americans, Coyote. These are the figures we may know. But every culture that worships authority will breed a Punch-like, anti-authoritan resister. Yin and yang -- it has to happen. The Germans call him Kasper. Truth-telling and serious pranking are dangerous professions when going up against power. Bradley Manning sits naked in solitary; Julian Assange is pursued by Interpol, Obama's Department of Justice, and Amazon.com. But -- in contrast to merely human faces -- masks and theater can often slip through the bars.

Consider our American Kaspers: Charlie Chaplin, Woody Guthrie, Abby Hoffman, the Yes Men -- theater people all, utilizing various forms to seed critique. Their profiles and tactics have evolved along with those of their enemies. Who are the bad guys that call forth the Kaspers? Over the last half century, with his Bread & Puppet Theater, Peter Schumann has been tireless in naming them, excoriating them with Kasperdom....
*from Marc Estrin's Foreword to Planet Kasper*

Fomite
Burlington, Vermont

### The Empty Notebook Interrogates Itself - Susan Thomas

The Empty Notebook began its life as a very literal metaphor for a few weeks of what the poet thought was writer's block, but was really the struggle of an eccentric persona to take over her working life. It won. And for the next three years everything she wrote came to her in the voice of the Empty Notebook, who, as the notebook began to fill itself, became rather opinionated, changed gender, alternately acted as bully and victim, had many bizarre adventures in exotic locales and developed a somewhat politically-incorrect attitude. It then began to steal the voices and forms of other poets and tried to immortalize itself in various poetry reviews. It is now thrilled to collect itself in one slim volume.

### My God, What Have We Done? - Susan Weiss

In a world afflicted with war, toxicity, and hunger, does what we do in our private lives really matter? Fifty years after the creation of the atomic bomb at Los Alamos, newlyweds Pauline and Clifford visit that once-secret city on their honeymoon, compelled by Pauline's fascination with Oppenheimer, the soulful scientist. The two stories emerging from this visit reverberate back and forth between the loneliness of a new mother at home in Boston and the isolation of an entire community dedicated to the development of the bomb. While Pauline struggles with unforeseen challenges of family life, Oppenheimer and his crew reckon with forces beyond all imagining.

Finally the years of frantic research on the bomb culminate in a stunning test explosion that echoes a rupture in the couple's marriage. Against the backdrop of a civilization that's out of control, Pauline begins to understand the complex, potentially explosive physics of personal relationships.

At once funny and dead serious, *My God, What Have We Done?* sifts through the ruins left by the bomb in search of a more worthy human achievement.

11234522R00153

Made in the USA
Charleston, SC
09 February 2012